THE CLANDESTINE BETROTHAL

*The Eversley Saga
Book One*

Alice Chetwynd Ley

Also in The Eversley Saga

The Toast of the Town

A Season at Brighton

THE CLANDESTINE BETROTHAL

Published by Sapere Books.

11 Bank Chambers, Hornsey, London, N8 7NN,
United Kingdom

saperebooks.com

Copyright © The Estate of Alice Chetwynd Ley, 1967.

The Estate of Alice Chetwynd Ley has asserted their right to be identified as the author of this work.

All rights reserved.

No part of this publication may be reproduced, stored in any retrieval system, or transmitted, in any form, or by any means, electronic, mechanical, photocopying, recording, or otherwise, without the prior written permission of the publishers.
This book is a work of fiction. Names, characters, businesses, organisations, places and events, other than those clearly in the public domain, are either the product of the author's imagination, or are used fictitiously.
Any resemblances to actual persons, living or dead, events or locales are purely coincidental.

ISBN: 978-1-912546-59-6

> "The desire of the moth for the star,
> Of the night for the morrow,
> The devotion to something afar
> From the sphere of our sorrow."
> *Shelley*

Chapter I: A Visitor to Strawberry Hill

On a fine May morning towards the close of the eighteenth century a favoured visitor strolled with Horace Walpole, fourth Earl of Orford, in the gardens of Strawberry Hill, that extraordinary Gothic villa which Walpole had built as a summer residence at Twickenham.

Many visitors came to the house during the summer months. Talk of its oddities had spread abroad, and the general public was eager to view the unusual rooms, and the valuable collections of antiques, curios and paintings which they contained. Never averse to fame, Walpole obliged by throwing open the house to the public for a few hours daily, subject to a strict set of rules. Only ticket holders were admitted, and tickets must be applied for some days in advance. Walpole reserved the right to refuse admission, and never granted it to children.

But although he was willing to show the wonders of Strawberry Hill to the world at large, Walpole had no intention of exhibiting himself. No doubt it was a disappointment to many of the visitors that they were never allowed to catch a glimpse of "Horry", for his claims to fame did not rest entirely on Strawberry Hill. He was as important in the social scene as his renowned father, Sir Robert Walpole, had been in the political sphere.

He was known as the author of that blood-curdling Gothic novel, *The Castle of Otranto*. He was known much more as London's most diligent and entertaining letter-writer, a certain source of information on all topics of the day, both social and political.

There were a few people, however, who found favour in Horry's penetrating eyes, and these were granted the rare privilege of a personally conducted tour of the house. The gentleman walking with him at present was one of this number.

They were an oddly assorted pair. Horry himself was small and slight, elegant still in spite of the gout which had afflicted him for some years, and which caused him to lean on a stick as he walked. He was finely dressed in a suit of lavender silk with the waistcoat embroidered in silver, hose of partridge coloured silk, and with gold buckles on his shoes. In defiance of recent fashion, he wore a wig combed straight back from a high, pale forehead which accentuated the piercing quality of his dark eyes.

In contrast his companion was tall, and wore his own thick auburn hair in one of the new, careless-seeming styles. He was quietly dressed, but the olive green coat and buckskin breeches were cut in the first style of fashion, for this was the Honourable Hugh Eversley, known to fashionable London as the Beau.

In his own way, Beau Eversley was as outstanding as Horry himself. His clothes were the envy of every aspiring dandy, his horses the admiration of every whip, his amours the subject of half the town's gossip. At twenty-seven, he was still a bachelor, and eagerly pursued by every match-making mama who ever brought a daughter up to London for the season. So far, all this effort had been wasted. The Beau generally seemed to prefer the company of opera dancers and actresses to that of even the most beautiful and talented females of his own circle. Occasionally, he had been known to permit himself a little light dalliance with one of the latter group, but even the most sanguine parent had never dared to suppose him serious in his attentions.

A great deal of this was, of course, known to Horace Walpole. It was his purpose in life to know such things, and to comment upon them in writing for the benefit (as he himself put it) of posterity. So he did not ask Beau Eversley about his personal affairs, but instead concentrated on gleaning news of the rest of the Eversley family.

"I declare it is an age since I saw your dear mother," he said, reaching out a white hand towards a spray of purple lilac, and sniffing delicately at the bloom. "How does she go on? She was always a favourite with me, as you will see by the miniature of her which I showed you in my special cabinet. So lively a spirit! And in person so captivating, with hair of that rich colour which you, my dear Hugh, inherit."

"We all have it," drawled Hugh Eversley. "In my sister Evelina it's plain red — although Cunningham married her in spite of it. As for my mother, sir, thank you, she is well, and as busy as ever, doing nothing."

"I must really pay your parents a visit when I am next in town. Perhaps they will like to come to me at Berkeley Square for dinner one evening? I believe Mrs. Cunningham is now the mother of two children. What of your other sister — the younger one? Let me see, her name is —"

"Georgiana," supplied Hugh. "She is at present languishing in a young ladies Seminary not more than a mile or so from here, no doubt up to some devilment or other, if I know her," he added with a rueful smile. "As a matter of fact she is to leave Miss Fanchington's care for good in a few days' time. I don't know who will be the better pleased — Georgy at being let loose on the Polite World, or Miss Fanchington at getting rid of what must surely be her most troublesome pupil."

Horace Walpole laughed in his pleasant light voice. "Your sentiments are what one might expect from a brother, my dear Hugh. I doubt if they do justice to the young lady. Had I known that she was lodged so close to me, I would have invited her to Strawberry Hill. I dare say she would have been glad to find some diversion to relieve the tedium of academic life — even so tame a diversion as a visit to an old man who has little to offer in the way of entertainment."

"Such modesty will not do, sir. You must know that Strawberry Hill draws the crowds as surely as Ranelagh or Vauxhall. But you are right in thinking that my sister finds the academic life tedious. The last time I saw her she was eloquent on the subject of the particular dress which all Miss Fanchington's pupils are required to wear. I must say in fairness," he added, reflectively, "that I thought her complaints justified. A dowdy grey woollen gown, shapeless, and quite unrelieved by any softening touches, crowned by a hideous mob cap, more suited to a dowager than a young girl." He paused. "But I don't wish to bore you with my family affairs. Perhaps we should return to the house, for I must not make you walk too far."

"You are very good, but my old enemy the gout does not trouble me much at present. You know my dear Hugh, an insignificant man that grows old wants something to give him a little importance; and with my meagre figure, what with its being a little respectable and what with its being a little comical, I find that gout does not at all succeed ill with me."

The whimsical bravery of this speech brought an acknowledging gleam to Beau Eversley's hazel eyes. He knew that the elderly man beside him often suffered severe pain, but evidently it could not blunt his irrepressible sense of humour.

"Very fine, sir," he began. "I could wish —" He broke off suddenly, laying long, tapering fingers on Horry's arm in a warning gesture. His sharp eyes had detected a movement among the trees on their left. The next moment all traces of indolence dropped away from him. He sprang forward into the trees. There was a short scuffle, and presently he emerged, dragging a small, grey figure with him.

"Let go!" panted the victim. "You're hurting me!"

Beau Eversley dropped his hands.

"Well, I'm damned!" he exclaimed, for once betrayed into amazement. "If it isn't a female!" He turned to Walpole. "I've heard much of the marvels of Strawberry Hill, sir, but this is the first I knew of nymphs haunting your groves."

At this point, the nymph let out a yell of pain. In the recent struggle she had lost her headgear, and now her black curls were caught fast in the branches of a tree. She struggled vainly to free herself.

"Allow me." With deft fingers, Beau Eversley carefully released the black ringlets, and then stooped to retrieve her cap. He handed it to her with a slight, ironic bow.

She took it, blushing, and stood for a moment without speaking.

"I think, madam,' said Horace Walpole, gently, "that we have not met before."

"No." The red deepened in her cheeks. "No — I — must ask your pardon for my intrusion, but the fact is —"

An ironic smile twitched Hugh Eversley's mouth. In his experience this phrase was usually the forerunner of some fabrication or other. He studied the girl thoughtfully. She was very much of his sister Georgiana's age, but slighter in build. Dark, dreamy eyes looked out from an attractive oval face which, at the moment, although flushed, had still a touch of piquancy about it. His glance travelled to the shapeless grey gown and the large cap which she was twisting nervously in her slim fingers, and a flash of recognition suddenly showed in his eyes.

"You are from Miss Fanchington's Seminary, are you not?" he asked.

She nodded, and swallowed. "Yes, sir. I — I chanced to be passing this way, and had a sudden fancy to see — to see —" she paused, and turning to Horace Walpole, finished in a rush — "your famous house, Mr. Walpole — that is — my lord. All the world talks of it, and I had only ever seen it at a distance, when passing along the highway in a closed carriage. Oh, I know I should not — it was very wrong of me, and indeed I beg your pardon —"

"But my dear young lady," interposed Walpole, gently, "had you requested it in the usual way, I would gladly have sent you a ticket to view the house. As it is, I do not quite know how you managed to gain access to the grounds. Did no one stop you at the gate?"

"I did not enter by the main gate. I found a side entrance where two gardeners were working, and I —"

"Do not tell me," said Horace Walpole, in pained tones, "that my workmen admitted you against all instructions to the contrary. Really, this is too much! Not that there could be the least objection to your visiting my house in the usual way, my dear Miss — I fear I have not your name?"

"Fyfield," supplied the young lady nervously, "Susan Fyfield, if it pleases you, sir."

Walpole executed a graceful bow. "My name you already know, Miss Fyfield; and this is a dear friend of mine, Mr. Eversley."

Susan nodded. "Yes, I know."

Beau Eversley lazily cocked an eyebrow. "You know? How can that be? To my knowledge, we have not met before."

"I know your sister, Georgiana," explained Susan, her eye avoiding his. "And you came once to visit her at the seminary. I saw you then."

"Did you? I hope you may not think it ungallant of me, but I have no recollection of that occasion."

It was said ironically, and once again the quick colour flooded Susan's cheeks.

"You did not see me, but I saw you, Mr. Eversley. I — we — that is to say, some of the girls were watching your arrival from an upstairs window."

Again the ironical smile twitched his lips, "Ah, yes! For a moment I was forgetting the insatiable curiosity of the fair sex. Miss — er — Fyfield. I am happy to think that my visit provided you all with some small entertainment."

"If you were ever at school," returned Susan, with more spirit than she had so far shown, "you will remember that almost any diversion is welcome to relieve the tedium."

He bowed. "I am answered. You hear that sir? I can be rated as a welcome diversion only when life is too tedious to be borne. I congratulate you ma'am. You certainly depress my pretensions most successfully."

"Oh but I did not mean —" She stole a quick shy glance at him, and a dimple appeared. "It is too bad of you Mr. Eversley! You are in jest, and I thought for a moment you were truly vexed with me."

"You are forgetting that I have two sisters. I am quite used to receiving the odd kind of compliment which you have just paid me. But won't Miss Fanchington be getting anxious about your absence? I take it that she was not in your confidence about this morning's exploit?"

Susan shook her head. The gesture reminded her that her hair was considerable disorder, and she put up her hands to try and smooth it down.

"No — I must return at once or I shall be missed." She turned to Horace Walpole with a graceful curtsy. "Permit me to take my leave of you, sir, and pray pardon my intrusion. I — it was very wrong of me, I know, but I do hope you will not feel it necessary to report my misdemeanour to Miss Fanchington."

"I have my share of faults, Miss Fyfield, but I do not number among them the trick of informing on a young lady. Particularly one who — if you will pardon an old man's gallantry — has sufficient charm of person and manner to make one forget an even greater offence." His keen eyes studied her thoughtfully, and a slight frown of concentration wrinkled his brow. "We have not met before, of that I am certain; yet you put me in mind of someone. Fyfield — I do not recall the name."

"No, my lord I do not think you would know my name. My parents died when I was a baby, and I live with my widowed aunt, Mrs. Fyfield. That is to say, I stay with her and my cousin Cynthia during the holidays."

"Somewhere close at hand, perhaps?"

Again Susan shook her head. "No sir, in London. But if you'll forgive me, Mr. Walpole — Mr. Eversley —" She prepared to curtsy again.

"How did you come here?" asked Hugh Eversley. She balanced carefully on one foot, holding her skirt. "A farmer who serves the school with milk brought me part of the way in his gig. I walked the rest."

She nodded, sank into her delayed curtsy, and turned to go.

"Stay," commanded Eversley. She halted obediently. "I will drive you back. And while I fetch my curricle, I fancy you had better spend a few minutes before a mirror, if Miss Fanchington is not to suspect you have been up to some mischief." He turned to his host. "Can that be arranged sir, think you?"

Walpole readily complied, and Susan was handed over to the housekeeper. In a very short time, she found herself seated beside Beau Eversley in a smart, precarious-looking vehicle pulled by two very fresh grey horses.

For a few moments she sat rigidly in her seat, her fingers clenched tightly in her lap. He glanced at her in amusement.

"What is amiss? Are you afraid your schoolmarm will have discovered your absence, and be waiting with the birch?"

Susan shook her head. "She doesn't use one."

"I didn't seriously suppose she did. I understand there are punishments, however."

"Oh, yes. But I was not thinking of that — I was not thinking of old Fanny at all, as a matter of fact."

"Old Fanny?" he echoed, with a laugh. "Yes, of course, I've heard Georgy use the nickname. Then what else was it that could give you that apprehensive look? Mr. Walpole will keep his word, you know — he'll not complain of your conduct."

"It wasn't anything like that. But the horses are so high spirited," confessed Susan, reluctantly. "I wondered for a moment if we might be overturned; and then I saw, of course," she added, hastily, "that you could manage them."

He turned to face her, his tawny eyebrows lifted. "You saw — that I could manage them! Once again, child, you set me down. You must know that I am considered a — tolerable whip."

"Oh, yes, I do know! Much better than tolerable! Georgy has told me of all your exploits. I am sure there must be nothing you cannot do well. I did not mean to suggest — only I have never been in a vehicle like this before, and it seemed a little dangerous —"

"It would do, after the farmer's gig. Very well then, you are forgiven, and I am suitably mollified. I feel I must mention, by the way," he added, "that you'd best not pay too much attention to what Georgy says of me. You must allow something for sisterly partiality."

"She is certainly very proud of you," agreed Susan. "Sometimes she tells us stories, in the dormitory, after the lamps are extinguished — she told us how you won the race to Brighton with an injured muscle in your arm — and how —"

"Does she so?" interrupted the Beau grimly. "It seems I must have a word with that young woman. She gives every promise of becoming a first rate bore."

"Oh, no," protested Susan. "We do so enjoy hearing her stories, truly! You see, so little that is interesting goes on at school."

"Hence today's escapade, I imagine."

She was silent. He looked towards her again, this time searchingly.

"You know," he said, slowly. "I may be doing you an injustice, but that story you told Mr. Walpole failed to convince me. There was some other explanation of your presence at Strawberry Hill, was there not? I feel certain that you did not go there just to see the house."

"You are mistaken, sir. I — I did. That was my only reason."

He tried again, but could get no other answer. But he noticed that she avoided his eyes, and felt convinced that she was lying.

And so she was: but how could she tell him that she had gone to Strawberry Hill today not to see the house, but to catch a glimpse, however distant, of Beau Eversley?

Chapter II: News of a Betrothal

"It would be idle to pretend," remarked Miss Fanchington judicially, "that your time with us has been spent entirely profitably."

Trained by a long apprenticeship with the back-board Susan sat erect in her chair, her hands folded primly in her lap.

"Yes, Miss Fanchington," she answered dutifully.

"Your proficiency at needlework and the pianoforte leaves much to be desired," went on the schoolmistress. "Your knowledge of the French language is imperfect, and your understanding of mathematics decidedly limited."

"Yes, ma'am."

"You have a sufficient grasp of your own language, however," Miss Fanchington conceded, fair-mindedly, "to write a tolerable letter, and to derive some benefit from the works of our great writers. I do not entirely despair of you on that head."

"No, ma'am."

"But undoubtedly your greatest talent, Susan, is for getting into scrapes." She broke off, and frowned. "I cannot believe that this is due to any lack of principle in you. In general, your character is good — however there is an unfortunate impetuosity in your disposition which impels you toward rash and unconsidered actions. This tendency, coupled with a strong imagination, must eventually bring you into serious trouble if you do not learn to deal with it firmly. While you have been in my care, I have tried both to show you the error of your ways, and to guard you from the consequences of them. In the future, that duty will devolve on your aunt, Mrs. Fyfield."

"Yes, ma'am."

"But it is with yourself, Susan, that the remedy ultimately lies." Miss Fanchington leaned forward a little in her chair, and some of the formality went out of her manner. "Think, my child, before you act — think not once, but twice; and if ever you should stand in need of a friend, remember that I am here."

Susan gulped. During the ten years she had spent in the seminary, she had thought of Miss Fanchington in many ways, but never as a friend. The idea was unnerving.

She managed to stumble through a short speech of thanks, however; and presently had shaken hands for the first and — she devoutly hoped — last time, with her schoolmistress.

After that she had only to take her place in the ancient travelling chaise waiting outside the door, watch while her corded trunk was safely bestowed, and wave frantically to the girls who were gathered round the windows of the school. Everything happened exactly as it always did when she went home for the holidays: the only difference was, that this time she was never to return. Schooldays were over, and her life in the world outside just beginning.

During the drive to London, which occupied a little under two hours, she speculated about this new life, and sighed a little for the old. She would miss the other girls, especially Georgiana Eversley, whose impish vitality had made her a general favourite. Most of all, she would miss Georgy's anecdotes of her adored brother, mostly told in whispers after the lights had been turned down in the dormitory. Perhaps this had been part of the magic for Susan, this atmosphere of conspiracy. Once or twice, after her friends had dropped off to sleep and all was still in the darkened room, Susan had crept from her bed and gently eased back a shutter, admitting a shaft of moonlight. She had gazed out into the night, drifting away into the realms of make-believe with Beau Eversley at her side: until one of the girls had stirred and uttered a sleepy grumble, when Susan had closed the shutter, and slipped quietly back to bed.

Whatever the future might hold, it was unlikely that she would see very much of Georgy. Susan's aunt lived on the fringe of the fashionable world in which the Eversleys moved. There had been the usual promises to meet, and Georgiana had insisted that she meant to send Susan an invitation to her coming-out party; but privately Susan wondered how much say her friend might have in the issuing of invitations for this much discussed, eagerly anticipated event. As far as she knew, nothing similar lay in store for her. When she had last been at home, no mention had been made of any formal introduction for her into Polite Society. In fact, she found it difficult to visualize her future life. She supposed that she would walk abroad with her aunt or her cousin Cynthia in the mornings, when the weather permitted; and spend her afternoons at needlework, reading or taking tea with their friends. This had been the pattern of her holidays in the past, with an occasional day's outing to enliven it. Possibly it might now include some evening outings too, since she was no longer a schoolgirl. There might be parties — though not on as grand a scale as Georgy's was to be, judging by her own account — and perhaps a visit to the pleasure gardens of Vauxhall or Ranelagh. Susan knew that her aunt occasionally went to these places, and she had heard much of the ridottos and masquerades that were held there, attended by people in all walks of life. It was even possible, she thought suddenly with a leap of her pulses, that she might one evening see Beau Eversley there.

Beau Eversley: could there be any future for her in which he did not have a part, even so shadowy a part as the one she had cast for him? She felt the tears starting to her eyes, and blinked them away, ashamed of her weakness. He had only ever been a dream-figure, she acknowledged, and perhaps in time would fade, like all dreams. But however severely she told herself of this, in her heart she remained unconvinced.

She was so deep in thought that she scarcely noticed when the fields gave way to cobbled streets lined with houses, and the teeming life of London surrounded her. She came to full awareness only when the coach turned out of Piccadilly into Duke Street, and stopped before one of the tall houses. The coachman pulled open the door, let down the steps, and helped her to alight.

A footman in a shabby livery opened the door, and received the luggage without enthusiasm. He then led Susan across the hall, which was rather dark, and opened the door into a small parlour at the back of the house. A lady of uncertain age was sitting before a small fire, inexpertly trimming a straw bonnet. She jumped up on seeing who was there, allowing the bonnet, ribbons, thread and needle to drop from her hands to the floor.

"Susan! So you are back! Welcome home, my dear."

She advanced on Susan, beaming, and planted a kiss on her cheek. Susan responded, for she was fond enough of her aunt, who had always offered her an easy, casual affection that made few demands on either of them.

"Did you have a cold journey? Lord, I think it's monstrous cold for the time of year. But May is ever a treacherous month. My dear Mama used to warn us always ne'er to cast a clout till it be out. Though whether," she continued reflectively, "the saying means the month or the blossom of the hawthorn tree, I cannot for the life of me decide. But come and sit down, child, and give me your news, and you shall hear mine."

Susan removed her cloak and bonnet, protesting that she had no news to tell. This was just as well, because Mrs. Fyfield was evidently bursting with hers, and began on it at once, without waiting for her niece to say more.

"Such a bustle as we are in at present! And worse to come soon, for there can be no reason for delay that I know of, and then there will be clothes to buy, and invitations to send out, and all manner of things to see to, as there always is on these occasions —"

"On what occasions, Aunt Hattie?"

"Why, of course, I have not told you! If that isn't just like me, as my poor husband always used to say. 'Hattie', he would say, 'you never can begin a tale at the beginning. Pray come to the point, and have done with beating about the bush.' Well, dear, to come to the point." Here she paused and gulped for breath. "As briefly as possible — your cousin Cynthia is betrothed!"

"Betrothed?" echoed Susan, in wonder.

"Yes. I am sure I don't know why you should sound so surprised, for she is a good four years older than you; and at one and twenty, you know, a female can almost be considered on the shelf! Indeed, I will confess that I was beginning to have some misgivings, for one needs a deal of money to put a young woman in the way of meeting eligible gentlemen. And as you are very well aware, child, in that regard I am not well placed — not well placed at all, I regret to say. Were it not for — but never mind that! The point is — dear Cynthia is engaged to a Mr. Beresford, a prodigious fine gentleman with an income of several thousands a year — not that it isn't very vulgar to speak of money, though how one is to avoid speaking of it when it necessarily occupies so much of one's thoughts, is more than I can say —"

"When did this take place, Aunt? I wonder you did not write and tell me of it."

"Well, Susan, you know I'm not much in the way of writing letters; and I very rarely put myself to the trouble of telling people things, because they always seem to find out quite satisfactorily in some other way. But as for when it happened — why barely a se'enight since! So you can plainly see that it was not worth the while of writing to tell you, more particularly since I am such a poor letter-writer, not at all like old Mr. Horace Walpole, whom everyone says is prodigiously gifted in that regard."

"I met him once," said Susan, blushing a little at that memory.

Her aunt was impressed. "Did you indeed? When I was a young girl, I used sometimes to see him at Ranelagh; but, of course, he never goes there nowadays, what with the gout and his age. In those days, one would meet all the *haut-ton* at Ranelagh: but it seems to me nowadays it isn't at all what it used to be — not at all."

"Oh, but will you take me there?" asked Susan, eagerly. "I should so love to go! I have heard how splendid it is!"

"Why, of course, child, if you wish, though it is nothing at all, I assure you — not like it used to be. But then nothing is, don't you agree? Oh, but of course, you would not know, for you have scarce seen anything yet, and I dare say you will think it all quite wonderful. However, we were talking of Cynthia's betrothal — we must keep to the point. This Mr. Beresford is well-connected, too. He is a third cousin — or is it a fourth cousin? — of a baronet. You can imagine how set-up my dear girl is with herself — especially after having felt just the smallest anxiety over the last year or so as to whether she was destined to remain a spinster all her life. However, all that is past, I'm thankful to say, and the only anxiety now will be on my part — though I would rather die than confess it to poor Cynthia. But the truth is, my dear, I'm at my wits end to know how to meet the expenses of the wedding!"

"I wish I could help, Aunt Hattie," said Susan impulsively. "Do you suppose —"

Mrs. Fyfield shook her head. "It isn't of the slightest use, child, though it's good of you to offer! But your inheritance is all tied up so that not even you can use it as you wish. But let's not concern ourselves with that," she added hastily. "For I always find a way to contrive, you know. I dare say I might take in a lodger when Cynthia is wed; there will be plenty of room in this house. However," she went on more cheerfully, "let's not tax our brains with such tedious matters. I must tell you what Cynthia was wearing when Mr. Beresford proposed to her."

She plunged forthwith into a lengthy sartorial account that was presently interrupted by the entrance of Cynthia herself.

Cynthia Fyfield was a well-built, shapely young woman with a face which would have been attractive but for a slightly heavy chin, and a mouth that was a little too wide. There was always a suggestion of self-consequence about her, but at present it was more noticeable than usual. She and Susan greeted each other calmly: there was no more than tolerance on either side.

"I wish you joy, Cynthia," exclaimed Susan, warming a little. "I was never more surprised in my life!"

"I'm sure I don't know why you should be," her cousin replied, distantly. "You must have supposed that I should wed before long."

"Oh, yes, of course! But there was never a hint of it when I was home for Christmas —"

"I had not met Mr. Beresford then."

"Tell me all about it," said Susan, plumping down on the sofa and patting the place beside her invitingly. "Come on Cynthia; pray do!"

Cynthia protested that there was not much to tell, but she seated herself beside her cousin in spite of this.

"You girls will no doubt wish to exchange your little confidences," said Mrs. Fyfield, indulgently. "I'll go and see the housekeeper about your room, Susan, for I declare I am quite tired of this stupid bonnet I have been trying to trim." She picked it up from the floor where it was still lying and turned it over thoughtfully in her hands. "One must practise economy in my situation, I realize, but there are limits! I am quite determined to give this to the housekeeper, and bother myself no further with it."

"Dear Mama is so irrational," remarked Cynthia, when Mrs. Fyfield had left the room. "She talks a deal about economizing, without having the least notion how to set about it."

"But she does contrive very well," said Susan. "She can always manage to find what is needed in an emergency."

"I'll admit that she will sometimes hit on the most ingenious ways of raising money," admitted Cynthia. "But it is all so distasteful to me, and if only she would at all times live within her income, such undignified shifts would not be necessary."

"But never mind my aunt!" cried Susan impatiently. "Tell me about your betrothal to Mr. Beresford."

"What shall I tell you?" asked Cynthia, with an indulgent smile.

"Everything! Where you met, and when — and how — what he is like — what he said when he proposed to you—"

"Lud — we shall be here all night if I tell you the half of what you want to know! Well, briefly, we met at a private ball at Mrs. Hibbert's in January. He is related to the Hibberts in some way, and had lately come to live in London. As you know, Lydia Hibbert is a friend of mine, so it was natural that I should often encounter him at their house. Before long, he was paying me marked attentions; and he actually made his proposals," concluded Cynthia, in a smug tone of voice, "six days ago, to be precise."

"But how did you feel about all this?" exclaimed Susan. "You tell it all so calmly! Weren't you in transports of joy, ready to dance and sing and do all manner of wild things?"

"My dear Susan, that kind of thing is all very well in novels, of which you've evidently been reading far more than you ought. In real life one's feelings are, I should hope, a little more under control."

"Mine aren't!" declared the younger girl emphatically. "And if yours are, Cynthia, then all I can say is that you cannot truly be in love with your Mr. Beresford! What's more," she added, glancing shrewdly at her cousin, "I don't believe you are, after all."

"When you are little older," replied Cynthia, repressively, "you will not talk such nonsense. Love, indeed! What should you know about love, I wonder? You have only just this minute left the schoolroom!"

Susan tossed her dark curls, free now from the hideous cap worn by Miss Fanchington's long-suffering pupils.

"I know all about it!" she retorted. "At any rate, I know a great deal more than you ever will! I know it can carry one to the heights of happiness and to the depths of despair —" She broke off, her cheeks flushed, and her dark eyes sparkling.

Cynthia looked at her with strong disapproval. "Upon my word, Susan, if I took what you said seriously, I should be bound to warn Mama that I considered you had come under some very undesirable influences at Miss Fanchington's Seminary! However, I know what it is. It is simply that you are jealous because I am engaged to be married."

"Nothing of the kind!"

"Do not trouble to dissemble, child. I shall not hold it against you," promised Cynthia, magnanimously. "A certain rivalry is only natural between sisters — for we have been brought up as sisters after all. I am sure it is perfectly understandable that you should be a little jealous of me."

"But I am *not* jealous of you at all!" protested Susan, becoming heated. "There's no reason why I should be!"

"Oh, come!" replied Cynthia, in a pitying tone. "You cannot expect me to believe that! Marriage must be every woman's aim; and you don't care to think that I am already betrothed, while you may have to wait some years yet before you are so fortunate — if, indeed, you should be. I could see, when I first came into the room just now, that you were not quite pleased with my news. But do not worry, my dear cousin," she added, consolingly, "when I have my own establishment, I shall ask you to stay with me, and then we will soon put you in the way of finding a husband."

To Susan, this was the last straw. Forgetful of Miss Fanchington's recent warning, she plunged into speech without pausing to think even once.

"Thank you, Cynthia, but there is no occasion for you to trouble yourself in the matter! I am already betrothed!"

Chapter III: An Evening at Ranelagh

"Of course it is nonsense," said Cynthia. "She says these things for effect — you know very well how it is with Susan, Mama."

"To be sure, my dear, yes — she was ever an impetuous and imaginative child. But don't you see," went on Mrs. Fyfield, doubtfully, "that is just the very reason why I wonder if there may not be something in it, after all? She says she has been secretly engaged for some time — and knowing how she rushes headlong into things, it could very well be true!"

Cynthia shook her head decidedly. "No: if it were true, she would tell us the gentleman's name."

"Yes, but suppose some unscrupulous person may have got to know her, and persuaded her to a secret engagement — she is a very considerable heiress, you know, and though I tell no one anything of our private affairs, these things do sometimes leak out."

"You are most discreet, Mama," remarked Cynthia, with a curious look at her parent. "I often wonder at it, for no one could say you are a woman of few words!"

"I may talk, child, but I never talk of anything that matters," explained Mrs. Fyfield. "Your father used to say so, and it drove him quite wild, poor dear! However, let us keep to the point. Someone may have heard that Susan is wealthy, and have set himself to captivate the child."

"What, while she was at the seminary?" asked Cynthia, scornfully. "You cannot have a very clear notion of what life is like there, Mama. Miss Fanchington is most strict, I assure you —"

"These things do happen, my love, in spite of strict guardians and rules. Why, I remember when I was a young girl, younger even than Susan — but never mind that," she broke off, hastily.

But Cynthia was not attending, or she might have remarked on yet another example of her mother's unexpected discretion. She was following a train of thought of her own.

"Mama," she said, presently, "I have never quite understood how it is that Susan is so wealthy while we have barely enough to live in the style of gentlefolk. Surely grandfather provided equally for both his sons, so that my father would have been as wealthy as hers? Or was there some special inheritance that came to Susan's father, and then, on his death, to Susan —"

"Lud, child, I have never troubled my head with such things as wills and legal settlements, but left all to the lawyers; and I advise you to do the same! All I can tell you is that your poor dear father was unlucky in his investments, and when he died I found myself in very sore straits indeed! But all that's past history, and doesn't help us to decide what's to be done about Susan."

"Personally, I propose to ignore what she has said," stated Cynthia. "It is just a piece of play-acting, I am assured, and if we don't refer to it again, she'll very likely admit presently that it was all a take-in. She has done that before, recollect, on other similar occasions?"

"Yes, but she's older now," objected Mrs. Fyfield. "And there was something about her manner when she insisted that she had been secretly engaged for some months past — something that convinced me the child was in love." She paused. "It was a kind of — of shining quality in her look, that one sees sometimes in girls who are newly betrothed. You may call me fanciful if you like, Cynthia —" intercepting a scornful glance — "but she could not have conjured up an expression like that without good cause."

"She may not be as innocent as we suppose," retorted Cynthia. "But I am certain there is no secret engagement."

"Do not say you suspect anything worse!" exclaimed her mother, in horror.

"Have no fear, Mama. Whatever you say I can't suppose that she's had any opportunity for — emotional entanglements — at the seminary. Possibly the dancing master may have aroused some foolish notions, but you can be sure that Miss Fanchington would make quite certain that there were no opportunities for dalliance. It is all in Susan's head, of that I am convinced."

"Perhaps I ought to have a word with her, though," said Mrs. Fyfield doubtfully, "Miss Fanchington, I mean."

"Had she known of anything, she would have thought it her duty to tell you, Mama. No, do as I say, and let the matter be. When Susan comes down from her room, let us meet her with calm faces and refer no more to her extraordinary outburst. We will go on exactly as we did before. I suppose," she added, as an afterthought, "she is to accompany us to Ranelagh tomorrow evening?"

"Tut!" exclaimed Mrs. Fyfield, "I'd forgotten about that — but, yes, assuredly she must go, for she was asking that very thing almost the moment she arrived, before you came into the room. It seems Ranelagh is one of the places she most wants to visit. Though, as I pointed out to her, it is not what it used to be when I was young —"

Cynthia stifled a yawn. "So I have heard you say countless times, Mama. But I think Mr. Beresford will be quite content, as long as the weather continues fine. Like Susan, he will be seeing Ranelagh for the first time."

The pleasure gardens of Ranelagh lay beside the River Thames in the village of Chelsea, and could be reached either by water or over a well-lit road which ran straight from Buckingham Gate. On a fine evening, it was pleasant to make the journey on the river in the brightly painted boats which were manned by watermen wearing white coats over their red or blue breeches. Unfortunately, the watermen were notorious for their shockingly forthright turn of speech. No doubt it was this which decided Mr. Beresford to convey his party to Ranelagh by coach.

The choice turned out not to be an entirely happy one. The road was jammed with vehicles which hindered their progress and threw up constant clouds of white dust.

"For heaven's sake, Susan, wind up your window!" urged Mrs. Fyfield, coughing. "There is nothing to be seen yet, and we shall all choke to death!"

Susan complied, with a small sigh, and contented herself with smoothing the folds of her pink satin gown. This had been borrowed from her cousin's wardrobe, and hastily taken in a little in order to make it a better fit. It was quite three years old and therefore not in the very latest mode; but to one used to wearing Miss Fanchington's choice of dress, it represented high fashion.

"We must see that lawyer of yours, and persuade him to provide you with the necessary funds to set up a new wardrobe," Mrs. Fyfield had promised. "But that will take a day or two, and in the meantime you had best borrow something of Cynthia's; for I declare I positively will not take you to Ranelagh in that monstrosity of a white gown — more like a bed-wrapper, I am sure! — that Miss Fanchington thought suitable for evening wear."

Susan had agreed wholeheartedly with these sentiments. While she waited impatiently for the coach to move onwards to Ranelagh, she allowed her mind to dwell pleasantly on what she would buy with her allowance. Many of the girls at the seminary had talked endlessly of dress, and some had produced fashion plates from the Lady's *Monthly Museum*, showing what the well-dressed female of the moment was wearing. She wrinkled her brow, trying to call these pictures to mind. There was a vogue for lighter materials, she remembered: muslins, cambrics and lutestring, instead of the silks, satins and damasks that had previously been used for lady's gowns. Because of the war, so the magazines had stated, materials brought in from the Continent would be more difficult to obtain; but there was also a trend towards simplicity which had started in France, where to be dressed in rich materials was to declare oneself an aristocrat, and thus invite danger.

The coach moved on again with a jerk which set the plumes in Mrs. Fyfield's crimson velvet turban nodding. Susan felt her excitement mounting. Soon they would be there.

There were to be many more stops and starts, however, and it was growing dusk before they finally reached the gate, where Mr. Beresford paid their dues and led them into the grounds of Ranelagh.

Susan looked eagerly about her. The extensive gardens were laid out in gravel walks and smooth lawns, shaded by yews and elms. Coloured lights glimmered among the trees, and from somewhere close at hand the scent of roses floated across the evening air. On her right stood a large circular building, slightly raised above the level of the rest of the gardens. The light streaming from its unshuttered windows gave it the appearance of a giant lantern. Mr. Beresford kindly informed her that this was the Rotunda, where people gathered to hear the orchestra and the singers, to partake of supper in one of the elegant boxes, or simply to stroll round and round the floor gazing at the rest of the company.

Mrs. Fyfield was in favour of making straight for the Rotunda; but Susan pleaded to be allowed to walk just a little while in the gardens. Mr. Beresford lent weight to her request by also stating a preference for this course, so the party turned in the direction of an ornamental canal which lay on the other side of the Rotunda.

Susan exclaimed in delight as they approached it. An illuminated Chinese temple stood on an island in the water, its lights reflected in the ripples made by small boats which drifted past them, each carrying a lantern suspended on a pole.

"Oh, how lovely!" she cried, eagerly.

Several passers-by heard this, and threw an amused glance in her direction. One of them, a tall, elegant gentleman with a striking-looking dark female on his arm, looked not once, but twice, on the second occasion taking his time about it.

"Sue, how you've made people stare!" whispered Cynthia, peevishly. "I declare, that gentleman is quite rude — Oh!"

She broke off, as the offender turned his eyes away from Susan and sauntered on with his attractive companion. Cynthia touched her mother on the arm, and stared after the couple in her turn.

"Mama!" There was excitement in her tone. "Did you notice who that was, the gentleman who looked round at Susan's silly remark? It was none other than Beau Eversley!"

"Yes, to be sure, love, I believe you are right! Though I did not catch more than a glimpse of him, myself—"

"Yes, it was," put in Susan quietly.

"How do you know, pray?" asked Cynthia, sharply. "You can never have seen him before."

"But I have. He came to Miss Fanchington's once." Susan's voice trembled a little. "You forget that Georgiana Eversley was a pupil there, and a particular friend of mine."

"To be sure, I have heard you mention her name," said Mrs. Fyfield. "But I did not know that you were acquainted with her brother. He is reckoned a prodigious beau by everyone, you know; and I am sure for my part, I never saw a more handsome man!"

"I — I am not exactly acquainted with him —" began Susan, hesitantly.

"No, how should you be?" interrupted Cynthia, crushingly. She considered her mother's final remark tactless in view of Mr. Beresford's presence, and did not intend to prolong a conversation which she could see very well her betrothed did not relish. "I dare say he is unaware of your existence!"

Mr. Beresford managed to forestall the hasty retort that was trembling on Susan's lips by suggesting that, if the ladies had seen enough of the gardens for the present, they might like to go into the Rotunda and have some supper. This was agreed upon, and they retraced their steps.

After the twilight of the gardens, the Rotunda seemed ablaze with light and colour. Susan gazed entranced at the company strolling in groups round the floor, which was covered with mats to deaden the sound. The gay colours of the ladies' dresses and the quieter hues of the gentlemen's coats formed a bright rainbow which circled before her under the lights of the glittering chandeliers.

"You may well stare, my love," said Mrs. Fyfield, "and indeed, it is odd that people are content to pass their time walking round and round like so many tops. But it is quite the thing, you know! Everybody comes here, though perhaps not quite as they did at first. I remember when I was very young, my Mama telling me that Mr. Horace Walpole had said that the floor was all of beaten princes. That was because," she explained, "you could scarcely set foot on it without bumping into one of the royal dukes. However, even nowadays you never know whom you may meet with — only fancy our seeing Beau Eversley here, and with such an attractive female too! I do wonder who she may be — though I dare say she is someone not quite — well, you know, they do say that he keeps the most odd company —" She broke off abruptly, and glanced at Susan, whose face was slightly pink. "But such talk is not for your ears, child," she concluded, hastily. "Only look at that wonderful central column where the great fireplace is situated! Do you not admire the paintings, and those flower-branches of small lamps hanging from the pillars? Yes; I dare say that to you Ranelagh is quite the most amazing place you have ever seen! I'm so glad that we hit upon the notion of bringing you here."

Cynthia interrupted to say quellingly that the original idea of the expedition had been to show Ranelagh to Mr. Beresford, and not to her cousin. Mrs. Fyfield was immediately contrite; and began to point out the various features of the building to her daughter's betrothed, who received her information in his usual calm manner.

While the three of them were occupied in this way, Susan, finding herself ignored for the moment, again looked about her. She noticed that rows of boxes were set round the building, one at floor level and another encircling a gallery above. Inside each of the boxes was a table spread with a cloth for supper. Many of them were already occupied, often by couples who, even from a distance, looked as though they were behaving in a shockingly lover-like manner. Susan hastily averted her eyes from one box where an elderly and rather stout gallant was pawing a very young girl who obviously did not object to his attentions. She turned her glance instead briefly on the box nearest the spot where they were standing. Then she started, and blushed, for she found herself looking straight into the eyes of Beau Eversley. He was standing alone, leaning over the balustrade and inspecting the crowd through his quizzing glass. No more than a few yards divided them. She saw that he had recognized her, and tried to look away, but he held her glance with those twinkling hazel eyes of his. Before she could guess his intention, he had left the box and was strolling across the floor towards her.

Instinctively, she drew a little away from the others. They were still engrossed in their conversation, and as people were passing to and fro all the time, for the moment they did not notice that Susan was no longer at their side.

Hugh Eversley bowed slightly. "It's Horry Walpole's nymph, isn't it? I noticed you in the gardens, but could not immediately recollect where I had seen you before."

Susan curtsied, and gave him a shy greeting.

"So you have left Miss Fanchington's establishment behind you for the moment, Miss — er — I fear I cannot recall your name. Pray forgive me."

"Susan Fyfield," she prompted. "And I've left the seminary for ever, sir, thank goodness."

"So you are supposed to have attained years of discretion?" He briefly surveyed the pink gown, and nodded approval. "Yes, you do better in garments of your own choosing — if I may say so, of course — you gain a maturity and elegance which is impossible in Old Fanny's grey uniform."

"And yet," said Susan, with a dimple, "even this gown is not truly of my own choosing. It is —" she hesitated, unsure of her dignity if she owned to the truth — "it is only a borrowed one of my cousin's," she confessed, in a rush.

"The young lady in your party?" he asked, indicating the others with a slight movement of his head.

"Yes. Perhaps," began Susan, doubtful on this point of etiquette, "perhaps I ought to present you?"

"Another time, possibly." He did not sound eager for the honour. He glanced behind him. Susan's eyes followed his, and she noticed that the dark-haired female whom she had seen him with earlier in the gardens, was now standing awaiting him in the box he had recently quitted. She was studying Susan intently, and Susan was close enough to notice a certain hostility in her look.

"I have company at present." Again he gave the slight, careless bow which had introduced their conversation. "*Au revoir*, Miss Fyfield."

She stood for a moment staring after him until her cousin's voice at her elbow recalled her to her surroundings.

"Well! I declare! It is not at all fitting that you should be putting yourself forward in that way, more or less forcing Mr. Eversley to acknowledge you! Mama, I think you should speak to Susan, at once!"

Susan turned away from the box. "I did *not* force him to acknowledge me!" she retorted indignantly.

"Well, but I am sure you must have smiled, or bowed, or something — for you did say that you weren't exactly acquainted with him," Cynthia reminded her, tartly. "And I think the least you could have done, since he did come over and speak to you, was to present him to your family. You showed a shocking want of conduct, and I wonder that Mama should tolerate it!"

"Well, I dare say Susan was quite taken by surprise," remarked Mrs. Fyfield, placatingly. "For no one could expect that a man of fashion would bother to acknowledge a girl straight from the schoolroom whom he has scarcely set eyes on, before this. But no doubt his sister has been talking a great deal about you, and that is how he was able to call you to mind. What did he say to you, my love? It is a great condescension on his part, as you must realize."

"I — he—" stammered Susan, by now rosy cheeked — "He remarked on my — gown."

"On — your gown, child?" echoed Mrs. Fyfield, faintly.

"You mean *my* gown," corrected Cynthia. "And what did he say about that, pray?"

"Oh, I — I do not want to be questioned further!" exclaimed Susan, with a toss of her dark curls. "It was a — private conversation, after all!"

Mrs. Fyfield and Cynthia exchanged glances, the one puzzled, the other incredulous. By common consent, however, they dropped the subject, deeming it bad manners to inflict it any longer on Mr. Beresford. A similar inquiry was at the same moment being conducted in the box, though in a very different manner.

Beau Eversley and his lady had seated themselves at the same side of the supper table, very close together. He handed her a glass of champagne, and raised his own.

"To the sparkle in your eyes," he said, softly.

Very fine eyes they were, too, of a blue so deep that it was almost violet. She leaned forward with one elbow on the table, and rested her chin in her hand, turning to face him, so that one of her glossy ringlets fell forward. He set down his glass, and twisted his finger in the lock of black hair, at the same time cynically reflecting that hair of that particular hue must surely owe something to art. Now that he was so close to her, for the first time he noticed the tiny lines under her fair fine skin, denoting that she was not quite so young as might have been supposed. These observations made no difference to his interest in the lady. He still would not have changed her company for that of any other woman of his acquaintance — but, after all, he had known her only a short time, as yet too short to find her tedious, like the others.

"Only just now you were admiring the sparkle in another pair of eyes," she challenged him.

She had a full rich voice, with just a hint of an Irish lilt. He shook his head, and, releasing the lock of hair, took her hand and carried it to his lips in a practised manner. His eyes caressed her face.

"There are no eyes but yours."

"Very pretty." She raised the fan that was dangling from her wrist, and lightly tapped him on the cheek with it. "But who was she, the babe you were talking to?"

He shrugged. "No one of importance. A friend of my younger sister's."

"She's pretty," said the lady, her eyes following Susan round the room for a few moments. "Do you not admire her colouring?"

"If I do," he said with a drawl, "it is only because your own is very similar."

"Her figure is graceful," continued his companion, "and she carries herself well. I believe she might even appear quite creditably on the stage."

He laughed softly. "Where you know very well she would be outshone by one Maria McCann, the toast of Dublin, and of London, too."

"Not yet of London," she corrected him. "You must give me a little more time here before that can be true."

"All the time in the world," he promised. "But need it be spent here in Town, and in acting? I have a tolerable house in the country, or we might take one in Brighton, if you'd prefer it. I am open to suggestion."

"But I am not," she replied, softening the firm reply with a smile which dimpled her cheek. "Acting is my livelihood, I must remind you."

"That could be changed." He rested his arm along the back of her chair.

"For how long?" The smile was still there, but now there was a fixed quality about it. "I have not been long in London, but long enough to hear of Beau Eversley's amours."

"You should never heed gossips, my dear," he drawled, moving his arm until it just touched her barely concealed shoulders.

"No? Then what should I do?"

"'Come live with me and be my love, and we will all the pleasures prove'." he quoted, promptly.

She laughed, a soft musical sound that set a more rapid beat to his pulses.

"I could remind you of the reply to that. 'If all the world and love were young, and truth in every shepherd's tongue' — no, sir. Give up my acting I will not, for you nor any man. When you have all done with me —" her voice dropped to a serious tone — "I still have that left; my work, and my consolation."

"Who could possibly ever have done with you, enchantress? And what need have you of consolation?"

For a moment, the blue eyes darkened with suffering. "There are things in a woman's life — in every woman's life —" She broke off, resuming as if to herself — "Have you never speculated, Mr. Eversley, on the two faces of an individual? One face is for the world. Most people never see beyond that, to the other."

"I was obliged to keep company with the philosophers in my youth. Do not, I beg you, expect me to renew that early and most uneasy acquaintance. There are so many more things we might talk about — or, better still, we need not talk at all. We could eat, for instance." He waved his hand over the table, which was amply spread with meats and choice fruits, and had a basket of dark red roses as a centre-piece.

She turned a vivid look upon him, all trace of her former grave manner completely vanished.

"Yes — we will eat a little, and drink a little —"

"And perhaps even love a little," he finished, softly, taking up his glass again.

Chapter IV: A Surprise for the Beau

A few days later, Beau Eversley looked in at his parents' house in Curzon Street. He was greeted enthusiastically by his sister Georgiana, who flung her arms about him in abandon.

"Steady!" He kissed her lightly on the cheek, and prudently removed the lapels of his well-tailored coat from her clutches. "I've no wish to look as though I've been in a bear-garden." He held her at arms' length, surveying her with quizzical affection. "Well, I must say you don't look as though your years with Miss Fanchington had done you any lasting harm. What do you say, Mother?"

Viscountess Eversley lifted her gaze from the paper she had been studying. The frown cleared from her face as her eyes rested on her eldest son.

"She is well enough; but she will have to put by some of her hoydenish ways if we are to bring her into Polite Society. I am glad you are come, Hugh, for perhaps you can make her see some reason about this list." She tapped the paper before her. "It's too absurd! The child wants to invite every girl who was ever at school with her, to her coming-out party!"

"Why not?" asked Beau Eversley, straightening his cravat. "I shouldn't think anyone else will want to come."

Georgiana exclaimed in disgust and Lady Eversley gave him a reproachful glance.

"Don't quiz her, I beg! It only wastes time, and I do want to get something settled, for the invitations must go out within the next day or two."

"I warn you *I* don't look for the honour of one."

"Of course not! As though I am such a goose as to send a formal invitation, to my own brother!" exclaimed Georgiana, laughing.

"You do mean to come, though, Hugh, do you not?" asked his mother, sharply.

"It's more than I bargain for; coming-out parties are not much in my line," he replied, carelessly.

"Oh, but you must come!" insisted Georgiana. "All the family will be there — you couldn't possibly stay away, you can't be serious!"

"Even Fredrick and George are to come, although it means abandoning their studies for a day or two," put in Lady Eversley.

"What you should say, ma'am, is *because* it means abandoning their studies," corrected her son. "I can think of no other reason to bring two such unlikely starters as my brothers to do the polite to a gaggle of young ladies fresh from Miss Fanchington's tender care."

"They are very charming girls," said his sister, heatedly, "and there is no need for you to take that superior tone about them! We are all aware of your preference for quite another kind of female —"

"Georgiana!" The snap in her mother's voice made Georgy pull herself erect, as if she were still in Miss Fanchington's presence. "You will mind your tongue, miss, or you will spend the next few days in your room on a diet of bread and water!"

"Yes, Mama. I beg your pardon."

"So I should think. Let me remind you that a young lady of quality is never unmaidenly. I am sure you must have been told so, before this."

"Yes, Mama," answered Georgiana, meekly.

"Very well, then." Lady Eversley turned her attention to her son. "But I trust you are only funning, Hugh, when you say you do not mean to be at your sister's party. It is only right that you should, as you must certainly realize. Everyone has been invited — everyone of any significance, that is — and we are something short on gentlemen as it is." She paused. "Barbara Radley will be coming."

He shrugged. "So?"

She threw him a quick, appraising look. "Oh, nothing. Only last time you were in company with her, I heard that you actually danced with her twice."

"The old pussies have been busy, as usual," he said, stifling a yawn. "If they could not give an account of every bachelor's dances and every female's dress, God knows what they would find to talk about. Yes, now I come to think of it, I did dance with her twice, but it was only to avoid having to partner Miss Rumbold. If there's one kind of female I abominate more than another, it's the gushing kind."

"That's not all, though," persisted his mother. "I fancied there was a period about six months ago when you were paying her a certain amount of attention. Nothing marked, I admit, except to one who knew you well."

"I beg, ma'am, you will confine your attention to Georgiana's affairs," he replied, somewhat stiffly. "My own go on very well, I thank you."

"Now, don't get in your high ropes, my dear. Only I do think I should be able to drop you a little hint now and then. You know how very much your father and I would like to see you settled."

The Beau inspected his fingernails, but said nothing. "If you have a preference for the Radley girl, I am sure no one could be more suitable — birth, fortune —"

"And she is pretty," interposed Georgiana, coyly.

"I believe we were discussing your party," drawled her brother, pulling out his watch and consulting it. "In any case, I can't stay more than a minute or two. I have an engagement."

"Oh, very well!" shrugged Lady Eversley. "I suppose you will take your own way, as always." She turned her attention again to the list before her. "I don't know the half of these people, Georgiana," she complained, a trifle pettishly. "Who is Susan Fyfield? You've marked her name with a cross, I see."

"Oh, yes, she's —" began Georgy, but she was interrupted by her brother, who repeated the name, then chuckled.

Both Georgiana and her mother stared at him for a moment.

"You don't *know* Susan, do you?" asked Georgy, incredulously.

"In a manner of speaking, yes; and then, again, no."

"Well, if you're to speak in riddles, I have done!" exclaimed his sister. "Either you do know her, or you don't! Which is it?"

"Who *is* she my dear?" asked Lady Eversley, plaintively.

"Oh, she was my best friend at school — my very best, Mama!"

"Do I know her family? Fyfield, I think you said —"

Georgy shook her head impatiently. "No, I shouldn't think so. Her parents are dead, and she lives with a widowed aunt in Duke Street."

"Then I don't know them," said her mother, decidedly. "And I don't think we can very well ask people with whom I am not acquainted. There will be enough —"

"Oh, never mind that now, Mama! I want to know what Hugh means." She took her brother by the arm. "Do you really know Susan? Do tell me, Hugh!"

He shook her gently off, and inspected his sleeve in mock alarm. "I see you're determined to ruin the set of this coat if I don't tell you all. Very well. I met Miss Fyfield at old Horry Walpole's — you may remember, Mother, my telling you I had called at Strawberry Hill one day last month."

Lady Eversley nodded. Georgiana was silent for a moment; then she burst out, "But what was Susan doing at Strawberry Hill? One day last month, you say? But we were both at school, then, and I know she didn't have permission to go out, or she would have told me of it —" She broke off, frowning.

"There was certainly no permission given for this outing. The young lady confessed as much. As for what she was doing there — well, she *said* she wished to have a closer look at the house. I must admit I didn't find it an altogether convincing explanation."

"Wait a moment!" Georgy paused evidently turning something over in her mind. "There was one afternoon, I remember, when we were supposed to be walking in the school grounds, and Susan was missing — I looked for her, and couldn't find her anywhere. Naturally, I kept quiet about it, for fear of getting her into trouble — Oh!" she stopped as a sudden thought struck her. "And now I know why she went to Strawberry Hill," she finished, her eyes dancing with merriment.

"Then perhaps you will enlighten me," said her brother.

"Oh, no! You are by far too conceited already! But you actually spoke to her, then? Did she go to the house and ask for Mr. Walpole while you were there?"

He shook his head, smiling. "Nothing of the kind. She crept into the gardens unseen, and I surprised her lurking in the shelter of some trees, where Mr. Walpole and I were walking."

Georgiana laughed. "How very like Susan! But she didn't say one word to me of all this — though I understand very well why, in spite of the fact that in general we tell each other everything."

"You grow mysterious, my child," said her brother. "Pray explain yourself."

"Not I! That is Susan's secret. You must ask her yourself, when you see her at my party."

"Which you most certainly will not do," put in Lady Eversley, firmly. "Not only am I unacquainted with the girl's family, but she sounds a most unsuitable friend for you, Georgiana! A girl who can get up to such starts must be lost to all sense of what is proper."

"Nonsense, ma'am," interrupted Hugh. "I dare say you would be shocked to learn of some of the rum starts your own daughters have got up to in their time."

"Hugh!" exclaimed his sister, in horror. "If you dare breathe a word of anything I've told you in confidence —"

"What's this?" queried Lady Eversley, suspiciously.

"Nothing of interest, Mother," replied Hugh, soothingly. "One or two silly childhood scrapes still weigh a little heavily on Georgy's over-active conscience, that is all." He drew closer to his sister, and added, in a low tone so that their mother could not hear, "But I may find myself remembering something more recent, if you don't tell me why your little friend went to Strawberry Hill."

"You are the greatest beast in nature!" whispered back Georgy, with feeling. "But if you must know, she went there because I had told her earlier that you would be visiting Mr. Walpole that day."

"Good God!" said Beau Eversley, in a strangled tone.

Chapter V: Tears at the Party

The Honourable Georgiana Eversley's party was one of many that were given for young ladies of her age in that particular London Season. To attend one was to attend all. There would be the same fashionable company, the ladies expensively gowned in the new classical mode, the gentlemen wearing well-cut tail coats with the knee-breeches and silk stockings which were still *de rigueur* for evening wear. There would be an orchestra discreetly placed in a gallery or on a dais set above the ballroom which would be gay and fragrant with flowers. The guests would be received on the threshold by the young lady of the evening and her family, and afterwards they would pass on to greet other friends and acquaintances who were present. After a discreet interval, there would be dancing for the younger guests while the older women would sit gossiping in small groups, and their husbands disappear for a quiet game of cards with a few cronies in an adjoining room. Towards midnight, supper would be announced; the guests would range themselves around the flower-decked tables where glass and silver sparkled in the light of the chandeliers, and proceed to dispatch with greater or less alacrity the products of a famous catering house. In only one respect did Georgiana's party differ from all the others: it was to be graced by the presence of Beau Eversley.

To Susan, this was a new world. From the moment that she entered the huge room amid a buzz of conversation and the soft playing of the orchestra in the background, she felt both elated and shy. Everything was larger than life. Her friend Georgiana looked magnificent in a pure white gown, the emeralds in her ears setting off the living beauty of her auburn hair. She greeted Susan in her usual enthusiastic way, and thrust her towards Lady Eversley, who was standing at her side.

"Mama, this is Susan Fyfield, my very special friend."

Susan glanced in awe at the imposing lady in green satin with the ostrich plumes in her hair. Lady Eversley bowed slightly and smiled, but did not offer her hand. She repeated the civility to Susan's aunt, who had been asked as a matter of form; it would not have been proper for Susan to attend the party alone.

"Sue, I can't join you now, perhaps not for ages and ages!" whispered Georgy, hurriedly. "I must be here to receive all the guests, but one of my brothers will present some eligible partners to you when the dancing begins. Oh, and you will find some of the other girls from school somewhere in the room —" She glanced about her swiftly, then shook her head. "I can't see anyone at present — but no doubt you'll run across them! Now, where are those brothers of mine? Freddy!" She raised her voice just sufficiently to reach the ears of a young man of some fifteen years of age, who was standing a little distance away on his own, gloomily surveying the animated scene. "Freddy, come here a moment! I want to present you to a very particular friend of mine. Where is George?"

The boy turned his handsome tawny head, and approached a shade reluctantly. Under his mother's watchful eye, however, he did what civility demanded; shaking hands with both Mrs. Fyfield and Susan, and conducting them to two vacant seats not too close to the orchestra.

This duty performed, he lingered uneasily, too polite to make his escape immediately, yet at a loss for conversation. Susan saw his predicament, and wished to help him, but could not herself think of anything to say. It was left to her aunt to fill the breach.

"How very like your sister you are!" she began.

Fredrick Eversley looked towards Georgiana. "Lud, ma'am, d'ye really think so?" he asked, anxiously. "Never mind — perhaps I'll grow out of it."

"I'm sure I don't know why you should wish to," replied Mrs. Fyfield, while Susan laughed. "Miss Eversley is really an exceptionally striking young lady — such height, and so stately a carriage, and then that wonderful, glowing hair!"

"Carrots," muttered Freddy.

"I beg your pardon?"

He started. "Oh — I am sorry, ma'am. Not everyone admires the family hair, though — for my first few years at school, I was always known as Carrots."

"Oh, well, schoolboys!" said Mrs. Fyfield indulgently. "They will always be making jest of something or other — not that I know much of boys, for I never had but one daughter. Still, evidently they grew tired of the joke as time went on, for you said it was only at first."

"They didn't exactly grow tired of it," said Freddy judicially. "It was more that I persuaded them to think better of it by and by." He regarded his fists thoughtfully.

"I know just what you mean," said Susan with a twinkle, following his glance.

"You do?" He gave her a quick smile. "Yes, Georgy said you were a right one, always kicking up larks. But still," he added, quickly, seeing the look on Mrs. Fyfield's face, and afraid that he might be getting Susan into trouble — "a girl's notion of a scrape don't amount to much, especially when it's Georgy, who exaggerates beyond all bounds — so I expect it's all a hum."

...e off in some embarrassment, and looked across the ...where his mother and sister were waiting to greet two ...arrivals.

"Oh, look, here's Hugh at last!" he exclaimed, in satisfaction.

Susan's heart missed a beat, and she felt her colour rising as her glance followed the boy's across the room.

"But who the deuce has he got with him?" asked Freddy, puzzled. "Well, if that don't beat all! It's Prinney himself!"

The orchestra stopped dead for a moment, played a single reverberating chord, then was silent. Everyone in the room rose in deference to the Royal visitor.

"Prinney?" queried Susan, as she stood up in obedience to her aunt's signal.

"The Prince of Wales, my love!" whispered Mrs. Fyfield, excitedly. "What a prodigious honour for your friend, to be sure!"

This information made Susan transfer her gaze for a moment from Beau Eversley to his companion.

The Prince of Wales was some years older than the Beau, and not so tall. He was elegantly dressed in a blue coat and satin knee breeches, but his figure showed signs of the corpulence that was later to make him take to wearing corsets. His face, though handsome, already bore the marks of dissipation. To Susan, he could not compare with the man standing at his side.

She watched, like everyone else, as Georgiana sank into a deep curtsy. Prinney took her hand and raised her erect again, then retained it for a few moments within his grasp as he chatted to her, smiling. Presently, His Royal Highness released the hand with evident reluctance and turned briefly to speak to Georgiana's parents. He lingered only a few moments longer, then, with a general bow to the assembled company and a deeper, more intimate acknowledgement to Georgiana herself, he turned to go. Viscount Eversley and the Beau attended him from the room.

"Now I hope he won't take Hugh off with him!" exclaimed Freddy, as a buzz of conversation broke out once more. "I declare it will be a great deal too bad if he does!"

Susan's heart sank, and she realized just how greatly she had been counting on the opportunity of a few moments in Beau Eversley's company. She did not ask for much: simply to be in the same room with him, to catch a glimpse of him now and then, would be enough. She was not even sure that she wished him to speak to her, for conversation with him threw her into such confusion that she was liable, she felt, to say the first foolish thing that came into her head.

Their escort had been glancing restively round the room. "There's George!" he said, with satisfaction. "Pray forgive me, ma'am, for a moment. There is something I must say to my brother."

He escaped thankfully in pursuit of a youth with the dark auburn hair of the Eversleys, who was purposefully making his way to the card room.

Susan and her aunt sat for a while in silence, watching the company.

"It is not very agreeable to have no acquaintance here," said Mrs. Fyfield, at last, with a sigh. "My love, do look at that absurd creature with all the feathers in her hair and her gown clinging to her as though she were in a state of nature! Upon my life, I never did see anything more abandoned! But there, it is all the same, nowadays — one cannot tell what the world is coming to."

Susan murmured something, but she was not attending. Her glance was fixed on the door through which she hoped every see Beau Eversley appear. The minutes lengthened, without bringing him; and after half an hour had ... , she was obliged to accept the fact that he would most likely not return. The evening was spoilt for her. Now there could be no expectation of pleasure from it.

Susan's reluctant conversation caused her talkative aunt to look elsewhere for entertainment. She found it in a middle-aged lady who was sitting close to them, and was for the moment alone. The two soon struck up a lively conversation, leaving Susan to her thoughts.

Her attention was caught presently by hearing them mention Beau Eversley's name.

"Of course he is quite distractingly handsome, besides being one of the most eligible *partis* in town," remarked Mrs. Fyfield's neighbour, in a confidential tone. "But he is the most shocking rake, you know. There is always some opera singer or other — the latest is an Irish actress, they say, called Maria McCann."

"Well, naturally I have heard so, madam," put in Mrs. Fyfield, determined not to be treated as a country cousin. "One can't help hearing the gossip, though I declare people are monstrous ill-natured to spread such stories abroad; often on the most slender evidence. Come to think of it, I did see him myself," she continued, relaxing her high-minded attitude a little, "not long since, at Ranelagh one evening, with a very striking looking female on his arm. She had dark hair and a very pretty figure, though I would not have said she was in her first youth."

"That's Mistress McCann, you may depend on it," replied her neighbour, nodding. "My sister went to the play at Drury Lane the other evening, and it was just so that she described the actress. It seems she was a great success. My sister said all

"I will attend to it," Hugh promised. "George shall dance with her, for one, though he does not yet know it."

"She would be far more gratified if you were to dance with her yourself," said Georgy, with a sly look.

"Possibly. But it is no part of my plan to encourage moonstruck schoolgirls."

"You are severe, you unfeeling wretch! I wish now I had not told you — though you did force me into it, recollect. Poor Susan! I should not have allowed anything to persuade me to betray her secret!"

"Don't fret," he said, soothingly. "In an unflatteringly short space of time, your pretty little friend will have forgotten my very existence. Once she meets some younger men with whom she can compare unfavourably an elderly bachelor with a shady reputation, my day will be done."

"Do you think so?" she asked, doubtfully. "Susan is full of fun, but underneath it all, she is very romantical."

"Because she has seen nothing of the world, my dear Georgy," drawled the Beau. "Living in Miss Fanchington's seminary is very close to living in a nunnery, as I know you will agree. In such an unnatural atmosphere young girls' heads become filled with moonshine. She will grow out of it, you'll see."

"I do hope you're right. But meanwhile you will be kind to her, won't you, Hugh? And not tease her, or treat her too much as if she were a child? For she is sensitive, too, and I won't have her hurt — no, not even by you, Hugh!"

"Give you my word," he said, with mock solemnity.

She was quite content with this light-hearted promise; for she knew her brother well enough to realize that beneath his flippant exterior lay a kinder heart than many people suspected. And she was inclined to think that he was right about Susan.

Her feelings for Hugh were only the hero-worship of a young girl who had so far met no men more worthy of notice than the elderly clergyman who had preached to them every Sunday in church, and the silly simpering dancing master at the Seminary, who had been an object of ridicule to all the pupils. Now that she was in the outside world, Susan would soon forget her moon-dreams. They were something that Georgy, with her more robust nature, could not fully understand.

As soon as the dance ended, Georgiana found herself claimed by another partner; and it was not until she had been dancing some time that she noticed Hugh emerging from the card room with her brother George in tow, and Freddy following them at a short distance, evidently protesting.

"You know damned well, Hugh, that I don't care for dancing," George was saying as he tried to shake off his elder brother's firm grip. "Don't care for females, either, come to that — rather have a game of cards, any day, than dance with one of 'em."

"You owe a certain duty to your sister," said Hugh, sternly. "You must help to entertain her guests."

"Fustian! I dare say this Miss what's-er-name don't care for dancing, either." He stopped suddenly as a happy thought struck him. "Tell you what — why don't you ask her, Hugh? You cut a sight better caper than I do." The Beau shook his head. They had now approached quite close to the spot where Susan and her aunt were sitting. He lowered his voice.

"I am engaged to dance with Miss Radley," he stated.

"Oh, the devil you are!" replied George, loudly. "You make off with the prize while I am left to lead out a girl who can't get anyone else to dance with her! That's rich, that is!"

"Not so loud, you dolt!" warned Hugh, as he noticed that Susan's head was already turned in their direction. He propelled his brother relentlessly forward. "May I present my brother George, Miss Fyfield?" he said, smoothly. "He has an ambition to dance with you, if you should be willing to gratify it."

Susan could never see Beau Eversley without showing some slight signs of confusion: but at these words, a deeper blush than usual came into her cheeks. He eyed her in dismay for a moment. Could she have heard what George had been saying, and have interpreted it correctly? He dug his brother surreptitiously but competently in the ribs. Thus prompted, George suppressed a scowl and made his bow, at the same time requesting Susan for the pleasure of the next dance.

"Oh, I am very much obliged to you, sir," she answered, stammering a little. "But — but if you will excuse me — I do not much care about dancing at present."

"There, what did I tell you?" hissed George triumphantly in Hugh's ear. "Now may I go back to the card room?"

"You may go to the devil," replied Hugh, in the same low, quick tone. Aloud, he said to Susan, "My brother can only hope that you may be prevailed upon to favour him later on. In the meantime, can either of us procure you some refreshment? A glass of lemonade, perhaps?"

Susan declined hastily, her cheeks still hot. A slight frown appeared on the Beau's forehead, and he wished ardently at that moment for the chance of delivering a well-aimed kick at his clumsy younger brother. There could be no doubt that the girl had heard his words, and was smarting under them. However, there was nothing to be done at present, and he must go and claim Barbara Radley's hand for the next dance. He excused himself smoothly to Susan, George made his bow, and they both left her side.

Susan's hurt and angry eyes followed the Beau. She saw him move towards Miss Radley and stand for a moment in smiling conversation with her, before taking her hand to lead her into the dance.

After that, Susan could not tear her eyes away, though every glimpse caught of them among the other dancers was torture to her. The glitter of the huge chandeliers caught and blended the colours in their hair, so close was his tawny head to Barbara's golden one. He moved gracefully, with a suggestion of power held in leash; and every now and then he smiled into the blue eyes of the lovely girl who swayed beside him in time to the music. Once she smiled in return; and, catching sight of her face, Susan's heart sank. Never could she hope to compete with the sheer witchery of that smile, she told herself.

Suddenly, she felt she could bear it no longer. It was a stupid, wretched party, and she could not think why she had ever come at all. She felt the tears threatening; and hastily mumbling an excuse to her aunt who was deep in conversation again, hurried to the ladies' retiring room.

No one was there, even the waiting maids being absent for the moment. A closet door stood ajar. Blinded by tears, Susan rushed into the small room, pulling the door shut behind her. Then she buried her face in her hands and gave way to her grief and chagrin in a stormy outburst of weeping.

Chapter VI: The Wine Goes to Susan's Head

After a while, she felt better, and determined to leave the party at once. It was absurd to stay for a moment longer in a place where everything had conspired to make her feel miserable. She crept stealthily from the closet, in case there should be someone in the room beyond. Finding no one there, she bathed her face at the wash stand, and carefully smoothed her rumpled hair before the mirror. The pale blue-green muslin gown which she had chosen with such care to set off her black hair and creamy skin was now a trifle creased. She straightened its folds, and adjusted her silver gauze sash. Then she shrugged her shoulders. If she looked a sight, what did it matter? There was no one to care, and, anyway, she was going home.

"But not before supper, dearest!" protested Mrs. Fyfield, when this announcement was made to her. "I declare, I have a prodigious appetite — and, besides, it will look so rude! Of course, I do realize that you have not found much pleasure in the evening so far, on account of not knowing many people, and having no partners. But I think, if you had not gone away, you might have remedied that; for after you had gone young Mr. George Eversley came over, and inquired where you were. If you stay but a moment, my love, I am sure he will come again and lead you out to dance."

"He may come fifty times," said Susan, vehemently, "but he will not lead me out! No, nor his brother, either!"

Mrs. Fyfield stared. "You mean the Beau? Well, I must say, my dear, that I think that scarcely likely, for he has danced with no one but the Radley girl all evening. Not but what it was uncommon civil of him to come and speak to you, earlier on —"

"Oh, vastly!" said Susan, curling her lip, which had started to tremble ominously.

"Well, so I think, for there are a good many guests here, and most of them a deal more important than we are."

"I agree, and that is why I say they can go on very comfortably without us," retorted Susan. "I mean to go, Aunt, whether you wish to accompany me —"

"May I ask where you mean to go?"

The cool, amused tones made Susan spin round quickly to face the speaker. She knew it was Beau Eversley.

"I am going home, sir," she said, abruptly.

He raised his brows. "So soon? I was about to solicit your hand for the next dance." He turned to Mrs. Fyfield. "What do you say, ma'am? May I lead your niece out?"

"Oh, to be sure!" answered that lady, in gratified tones. "So obliging of you, Mr. Eversley — I am sure that Susan will be delighted, for she has not danced yet all the evening, and when one is young, you know, it is agony to sit out a single dance! But away you go, and I shall be quite content to chat with my friend here for a while."

He took Susan's hand, and, mesmerized by his smile, she allowed him to draw her a little way towards the dancers. Then she stopped, roughly pulling her hand from his light clasp.

"Whatever my aunt may say, Susan will *not* be delighted!" she exclaimed, heatedly, the colour flooding her face. "I'm going home, Mr. Eversley — I don't wish to dance."

"No?" He studied her flushed face, amusement in his eyes. "Do you know, Miss Fyfield, I am sorry to say that I cannot think you are a very truthful young lady?"

"I — I don't know what you mean —"

"I mean," he said, with a smile that robbed his words of offence, "that when we first met at Horry Walpole's you gave a reason for your presence there that seemed to me — shall we say improbable? And now you want me to believe that you have no wish to dance — again, improbable."

"You may believe what you wish," retorted Susan, compressing her lips defiantly.

He bowed. "Thank you. I intend to do so, but it is reassuring, of course, to have your permission." His tone changed. "Come," he said, coaxingly, "what is all this about? Are you having a slow time of it? I am sorry for that, and we will do our best now to remedy it — but we must take our places, for the dance is beginning, as you see."

"Oh, you treat me as if I were a child!" she burst out, her lip trembling.

He took her hand purposefully. "Come, ma'am, we are going to dance together now, and afterwards I intend to take you in to supper. I warn you —" as she looked rebellious — "I shall brook no denial. I am quite capable of carrying you bodily on to the floor, if need be."

"Oh!" She tried to sound indignant, but ended by breaking into a laugh. "Oh, you are — outrageous, sir!"

He looked down into a pair of brown eyes, which had suddenly begun to twinkle.

"And you are — charming, ma'am," he said, mimicking her.

She caught her breath as their glances met, and once again the colour flooded her cheeks. But she had no time to feel embarrassed, for at once he guided her expertly into the cotillion, and she was occupied for the next few minutes in watching her steps.

After that, it was all like a dream. The music, the movement, the nearness of this man who had always seemed as far removed from her as though he inhabited another planet, the touch of his hand in hers — all were intoxication to Susan's senses. She danced as if she were floating on a cloud, or had wings on her feet. She was altogether oblivious of everything except his presence; she failed to notice the covert glances, the nudges and whispers that passed round among the spectators, and even the dancers themselves.

Not so the Beau: he was too used to being the subject of gossip not to guess that tongues would be wagging at his expense. To be dancing with someone new and quite unknown in society — and a little schoolroom miss at that! This was a new start for Beau Eversley, indeed; but, whoever she was, she had better watch out for herself. That was more or less what the old Tabbies would be saying, he conjectured cynically. How disappointed they would be if they knew the truth; if they realized that for once the Beau was not pursuing his own selfish amusement, but trying to oblige a sister of whom he happened to be particularly fond. He frowned at this stage in his thoughts, his attention caught. Oblige Georgiana? Was that truly the case? He had to acknowledge that there was a little more to it than that. He had started out to oblige Georgy, it was true, but now his aim was to give some pleasure to the child at his side. He fancied he was succeeding, too. He glanced down at her. She was gliding through the dance as if her feet scarcely touched the ground, the pale oval of her face uplifted, her eyes dark and mysterious. She was a child, of course, not yet eighteen — and yet, he thought suddenly, she was a woman, with all a woman's mystery and allure. Perhaps he need not feel so self-righteous about the gossips. It might be that, as they had supposed, he was in reality pursuing his own selfish amusement, after all.

To go in to supper on Beau Eversley's arm was to perpetuate the dream through which Susan thought she must surely be moving at present. Both events had been quite outside even her wildest flights of fancy. In a daze, she found herself sitting next to him at the long, flower-decorated table which was loaded with expensive food calculated to appeal to every eye and palate. It was quite wasted on Susan, for she had no idea what she ate, and very little understanding of what was going on around her. On one occasion, she noticed her aunt smiling at her from a seat lower down the table; on another, Georgiana, seated at the head of it, leaned forward and caught Susan's eye with a knowing look which momentarily broke through her abstraction, causing her to blush and look down hastily at her plate.

But, for the most part, there might have been no one else present but herself and Beau Eversley, caught up in a whirl of bright stars which must eventually burst into flame.

"You are very silent," remarked the Beau, presently. "Are you still displeased with me?"

She shook her head, and turned a contrite look upon him. "I beg your pardon, sir — I fear I was impolite —"

"Perhaps I prefer you to be impolite," he said, smiling. "It gives you animation. Besides, one meets polite young ladies everywhere. There's nothing remarkable about them."

"But if every female answered you rudely, Mr. Eversley," she replied, dimpling, "then you would wish to meet one who was polite."

"Assuredly." He raised a quizzical eyebrow, his eyes twinkling at her. "Am I not a contrary character?"

A footman passed behind them to fill their glasses with champagne, and Susan fell silent.

"Tell me," said the Beau, in a careless tone, "what exactly was the explanation of your sudden outburst in the ballroom?"

She coloured slightly. "I would rather not talk about that," she said, in a low tone. "As long as you have forgiven me for my lapse of manners, pray let us forget all about it!"

"Of course," he replied reassuringly. "All the same, it would be a pity if you were to attach the smallest significance to the words of a selfish young blockhead whose one abiding passion in life is cards."

Susan shook her head, and picked up her glass, seeking a way to change the subject.

"What is this, sir?" she asked, in a voice that was not quite steady. "It doesn't look like lemonade."

He laughed. "The taste isn't the same, either. It's champagne. If you haven't had any before, you may not care for it very much. You must drink Georgy's health, presently, but there is no need to take more than a sip, so don't worry."

She conveyed the glass to her lips, and doubtfully tasted the champagne. Then she turned towards him with a delighted expression.

"Oh, I like it!"

Before he could intervene, she had tipped up the glass and drained it.

"I did not realize how thirsty I was!" she declared, naïvely. "And now I have none left to drink Georgy's health! Do you think I might have some more?"

He raised a quizzical eyebrow. "If I had realized you were thirsty, I would have ordered some lemonade for you instead. At the risk of being thought a dead bore, I feel I must warn you that it is wiser not to toss off champagne in just that careless style. However, we must hope for the best." He signalled to the footman, who approached bearing the champagne bottle. "The lady will take a little — a very little — more," he instructed.

A small quantity was poured into Susan's glass.

"May I beg you," said Beau Eversley, smiling down into her slightly crestfallen face, "this time to treat your wine with a little more respect?"

"Oh, yes — I had no notion — you see, I have never had anything but lemonade or ratafia, before!"

This soon became apparent, for in a few moments she began to giggle. The Beau looked at her sharply. She turned a brilliant smile and a pair of dancing eyes towards him.

"Oh, dear, I do seem to be doing all manner of outrageous things this evening!" she exclaimed, slurring her words slightly. "But isn't it odd — I don't care the least little bit in the world, now! I cannot ever recall feeling so — so carefree and g-gay!"

"That is capital," he replied quietly. "But I beg you to moderate your voice a little. There are always unkind people who are ready to gossip, you know, and nothing sets them off like the sight of a young lady — er — too evidently enjoying herself in company with a man."

Susan nodded with careful solemnity. "I w-will be very discreet," she whispered, placing a finger to her lips, "for I must not make people gossip, I know. They talk of you already — you and an actress called Maria —"

Although she was feeling more than a trifle hazy, his quick frown penetrated her consciousness, and made her break off abruptly.

"I must ask you to recollect what you are saying, ma'am," he said, sharply.

She opened her eyes wide. "Oh, now you are cross! Do you think I am — what is it you gentlemen say? — bosky? Oh, dear! What if I am?" She giggled again, though this time more quietly, then went on, "But I really cannot bring myself to care. And if you do not like to speak of —"

She stopped again, as he directed a warning look at her.

"But I dare say you are right," she continued, in a lively tone, but not quite so loud as before. "I must not tease you. All the same, I wonder would you object to telling me if — if you are in love with — with Miss Radley?" She gazed at him earnestly, as though trying to bring his face into focus. "I have a most — particular reason — for wanting to know."

"I think you should go home, Miss Susan," he said gently.

"So soon?" she protested, pouting at him. "But I have not yet drunk Georgy's health — and you haven't answered my question."

"I think you have drunk sufficient for tonight," he said, firmly. "Georgiana's health is not so greatly threatened as your own must be if you remain."

He glanced down the table to where his father sat, and was relieved to see that Viscount Eversley was just about to rise and propose the toast of the evening. After that, it would be possible to take Susan away without causing comment. He was quite indifferent to gossip himself, but had no intention of doing anything to draw it down upon the innocent child at his side.

Fortunately, his father's speech was short and to the point, and Susan showed no disposition to fidget or interrupt, as he had feared she might.

When the moment came to rise and drink Georgiana's health, he placed a firm hand under Susan's elbow. He was relieved to find that she was able to stand without swaying.

"Only one small sip!" he directed, in a forbidding undertone, as she raised her glass with the rest of the table.

She turned a look of sparkling defiance on him in answer. For a moment he contemplated taking the glass away from her; but once again he hesitated to bring her to the attention of the rest of the company. Then she shook her head slightly with a reassuring glance, taking only the tiniest sip before setting down her glass.

"You see!" she said, as they resumed their seats. "I obeyed you, after all."

"It will pay you better to do so always," he answered, grimly. "And now we may go. It will no longer occasion any remark."

She shook her head vigorously, and set her dark curls swinging.

"Not until you answer my question," she insisted.

"As I have no intention of doing so, we had better be prepared to sit here until you fall asleep," he countered.

"I do not feel sleepy in the least."

"Perhaps not. That will come presently. You would be well advised to leave before it happens."

"I see what you are at, but it shan't succeed, I promise you." She shook an admonitory finger at him. "You *shall* answer my question — and I intend to sit here until you do."

"Then you are likely to sit here alone," he said, in a brutal tone, "for I have no intention of remaining."

"You — you could not do that — it would be ungallant —"

"I do not feel particularly gallant at the moment."

"I don't suppose you do," she said, slurring the sibilants slightly. "Now if I were only Miss Radley — or M-Maria McCann —"

"If you were only my sister," replied the Beau, tightening his lips, "I should know how to deal with you."

"Tell me what I want to know," she insisted, leaning towards him in a way that almost threatened her balance, "and then I'll be quite willing to leave — when — whenever you wish."

He glanced covertly around him. At the moment, no one appeared to be paying any particular attention to his indiscreet companion. When they had first sat down at the table together, he had noticed that every eye was upon them. Most people had finished supper, and were now leaving the table. If he could only persuade Susan to leave quietly and go straight home with her aunt, there would be no harm done beyond her being pointed out by the gossips as Beau Eversley's latest flirt.

"Very well," he said, capitulating. "If it will keep you quiet, I may inform you that I am not in love with anyone."

"Not even with M-M —" she stumbled, even in her present carefree mood hesitating to repeat the name that had offended his ears.

Deliberately, he chose to misunderstand her. "No, not even you," he said, laughing. "Not as far as I know."

Her glance wavered for a moment. "But I did not mean — I was not going to say —"

"I have answered your question," he said, rising. "And now you must keep your part of the bargain. Are you ready to go home?"

She rose with a nod, and accepted his arm.

Most of the company had returned to the ballroom, but some now began to leave the party. With characteristic speed and smoothness, Beau Eversley united Susan with her aunt, and whisked them through the necessary leave-taking. He himself escorted them to their carriage, bowing over Susan's hand when he had seen her safely curled up in a corner.

"Goodbye, Miss Indiscretion," he said, in a low tone for her ears alone.

"So obliging!" enthused Mrs. Fyfield, from her own corner. "Such a delightful evening! I fear we did not thank Lady Eversley and your charming sister half enough! But then, we were obliged to rush away — as you say, Susan is monstrous tired, which is not to be wondered at, for she is not accustomed to late nights, evening parties and such like entertainments — but I am sure she enjoyed herself prodigiously."

"The pleasure has been all on our side, ma'am, I assure you," replied the Beau, with another bow. "Goodnight."

He carried Susan's limp hand briefly to his lips, before stepping back and closing the door of the carriage.

"I've said before, and I'll say again," remarked Mrs. Fyfield, in a gratified tone, "I never did see so handsome a man! And with such address, such charm of manner! My love, he certainly did seem to be paying you a deal of attention — though, to be sure, I would not have you refine too much on that, for they say he is a shocking flirt, and I would not have you taken in for the world!"

Susan heard her aunt's words through a haze of exaltation. The unaccustomed champagne, the heady delight of the Beau's company, the final shattering effect of the quick touch of his lips on her hand — all had combined to make her senses swim.

"You need not worry over me, aunt," she said, dreamily, gazing into space. "You need not worry at all. You don't need to tell me anything about Beau Eversley — I know all there is to know about him. You see, we are betrothed. But don't tell anyone —" She placed her finger on her lips, and spoke in a whisper — "don't tell anyone at all. It's a secret."

And having delivered herself of this bombshell, she promptly dropped off to sleep.

Chapter VII: Susan Confesses

Susan awoke late the next morning with a sense of something hanging over her head. As she hurried through her toilet, she tried to decide exactly what this could be. She had only a hazy memory of the events of the preceding evening, but two things were clear in her recollection. One was that Beau Eversley had actually danced with her and taken her in to supper: the other was that in bidding her goodnight, he had kissed her hand.

And why not? she asked herself, defensively. It was not so unusual for a gentleman to kiss a lady's hand, after all.

But when the lady might scarce be considered old enough to be an object of gallantry, and was, moreover, of little account in the Polite World; and when the gentleman was Beau Eversley — then, the affair assumed some significance. She hugged the thought to herself as she went downstairs to breakfast.

Her aunt and Cynthia were already at the table; and by the way they broke off their conversation as she entered, she guessed that they had been talking about her. The suspicion was immediately confirmed.

"Now, Susan," began Mrs. Fyfield, in what was for her a firm manner. "I want to talk to you very seriously indeed."

Susan sat down at the table unconcernedly, and helped herself to some bread and butter.

"What about, Aunt?"

"You may well ask," put in Cynthia, before her mother could speak. "Anyone would think to look at you that you did not remember what you had said to Mama last night!"

Susan paused in the act of conveying the food to her mouth. "What I said last night?" she repeated, puzzled.

"If you think to deceive us by pretending you have forgotten, I can tell you that it won't answer with me!" retorted her cousin, tartly. "And if Mama allows herself to be taken in, I shall be amazed, that's all I can say."

"But I really don't know what you mean, Cynthia, I assure you I don't. Aunt Hattie, what is she talking about?"

"Well, I must say you were more than half asleep when you said it, and afterwards you went right off to sleep, and had to be almost carried from the coach to your room. Try as I would, I could get nothing more out of you. So I left you to get into bed with the help of the housemaid —"

Cynthia made an impatient movement. "Mama, let us keep to the point. It is no use to say you don't remember, Susan. We want to know the truth. Are you or are you not engaged to Beau Eversley?"

Susan stared at her cousin in silence for a while. Then the colour flooded her face as all the happenings of the previous evening returned clearly to her memory. For a moment, she was tempted to continue the deception; it would certainly give Cynthia a good set-down. For once, however, she did pause to think, and wiser counsels prevailed.

"Of course I am not."

'Then why did you say you were?"

"Because — oh — because," stammered Susan, blushing furiously, "I thought it would sound — interesting, I suppose. I don't really remember."

"She did have some champagne," Mrs. Fyfield explained to Cynthia, "and of course she is not accustomed to strong liquor of any kind, as you are aware. But all the same —" she finished, with a frown, "I must say he did pay her a deal of attention, especially as she is not yet what one might call 'out', you know. To dance with her at all was a remarkable condescension — and as for taking her in to supper, and devoting his attention at the table almost exclusively to her — I thought it rather odd, at the time, but now I look back on it, I am bound to say that his attentions were more than one would expect in the common way."

Susan looked gratified, but said nothing.

"'Pon rep!" exclaimed Cynthia, angrily. "It is very difficult to know what to believe! A man such as Beau Eversley does not engage himself to an insignificant little schoolgirl with neither looks nor conduct — not unless he knows she is a considerable heiress, and he is in want of a fortune! And such, as we know very well, is not the case! Beau Eversley of all people does not need to marry for money."

"But can we be sure of that, my love? Perhaps the family circumstances may have changed —"

"Nonsense!" snapped Cynthia. "Such things get about in no time, particularly when they concern a man who has always been a subject for gossip." She turned to Susan, who had been standing silently by during this interchange. "Now, miss, we mean to have the truth. It's not the first time that you've informed me you are betrothed. I did not believe you, then, for I was certain that you said it to try and lessen the importance of my own recent engagement. I can see the reason for such a statement to me, for you have always shown yourself jealous of any advantage which I seemed to possess over you. But I must confess that I cannot so easily account for your telling Mama this story. Why should you seek to deceive her? It almost seems — although I cannot entirely credit it — as if you had accidentally let slip something which you had agreed to keep secret."

"I must say, child," put in Mrs. Fyfield, appealing to Susan, "that I agree with Cynthia. Of course, we both thought you were boasting when first you said you were betrothed, and we determined to say no more about it until you confessed that it was a take-in. But now — after what happened last night at the party —" She broke off, and turned once more to her daughter — "and there's another thing, Cynthia, that I must tell you, that makes it all very strange! This lady I was talking to, at the party — she said that everyone wondered why the Beau did not marry, and that some said it might be because he was secretly wed, or perhaps betrothed! Now, does not that all seem to fit in?"

Susan came suddenly to life, alarmed at the course of their surmises.

"Fudge!" she said, energetically. "You are going on in such a stupid way, so I suppose I had better tell you the whole! It is none of it true. Cynthia is quite right — she was being so vastly patronizing and — and superior about her own betrothal that I felt bound to set her down a peg. As for yesterday evening —" she blushed again — "I'm afraid it *was* the champagne after all. Mr. Eversley was prodigiously kind to me, but I expect," she added, reluctantly, "that he only did it to oblige his sister. I know he is very fond of her. And now please — please — do not let us talk of it any more! I am sorry to have made mischief, but it was only a take-in, as you guessed!"

They both stared at her consideringly for a moment. Then Cynthia pushed back her chair, and rose from the table.

"I tell you what, Mama," she stated, emphatically, "I should not believe her. I think she is concealing something behind this show of frankness. Perhaps you had better ask Beau Eversley himself whether they are betrothed or not."

"No!" Susan exclaimed in horror, flinging herself imploringly on her aunt. "Oh, no, Aunt Hattie, you will not — you could not! I assure you, it was all a hum — Oh, I swear it, on any solemn oath you wish! Only don't — please don't ever mention the subject to *him*!"

"Because you have promised to keep it secret?" taunted Cynthia. "And now that you have let the cat out of the bag he will be angry with you, I suppose. Confess now — why does it have to be kept secret? Is it because he considers you beneath him, and is hoping to be rid of you in time? Or is it —"

Quite distracted, Susan flew at her cousin, and would have struck her had not Mrs. Fyfield risen quickly to intervene.

"Susan! Recollect yourself — you are not in the schoolroom now! You had better go to your room, and stay there until you are more in command of yourself. As for you, Cynthia," she finished, as Susan turned to obey, "you should be ashamed to taunt the child in that way."

Susan turned blindly away, and flung out of the room. But as she closed the door behind her she heard her aunt saying to Cynthia: "All the same, I think there may be something in what you say; and though I dislike excessively the notion of approaching him on such a subject, I think perhaps I ought to speak to Mr. Eversley."

Angry tears scalded her eyes, and she rushed headlong upstairs to fling herself face downwards on the bed. What a fool she had been! It was just as Old Fanny had warned her — if only she had taken the trouble to think first before boasting to Cynthia of a fictitious betrothal, none of this would have happened. She could not blame herself in quite the same way for what she had said last night — that had been different: neither was the heady sensation she had experienced in the coach attributable only to the unaccustomed champagne. It was quite as much due to the effect on her of Beau Eversley's company, and his distinguishing notice. She had spoken the words in a dream; and as part of a dream they had drifted from her consciousness, until she had been reminded of them this morning. It was all so dreadful — and now her hateful cousin was trying to persuade Aunt Hattie to go and question the Beau.

She sat up suddenly. She must stop this — but how? She had made one appeal to her relatives, and she recognized the futility of making another. The more she protested, the more likely it was that they would think her falsehood was the truth, after all. Contrary creatures, she thought angrily. When she had lied, they had refused to believe her; and now that she was telling the truth, they still thought she was pretending.

Perhaps they would not go to see Beau Eversley, after all, she thought, taking heart a little. Then she remembered her aunt's final words just as she had been leaving the room, and the faint hope died. There had been a note in Aunt Hattie's voice which Susan knew of old, and which had usually meant that action would be taken, however reluctantly, because Mrs. Fyfield had recognized a duty which ought to be performed.

She must face the fact that Aunt Hattie would go to Beau Eversley and ask him for the truth. What would he think of her when he heard the story she had told?

Her tears checked suddenly, and a wave of horror swept over her as a most unwelcome thought occurred to her. Merciful heavens! He might even think that she had told her aunt she was betrothed to him in order to force him into a proposal of marriage!

This must not be. There was only one thing to be done. She must see him first herself, and explain the whole affair to him as best she could. Anything would be better than for Aunt

Hattie to confront him, and ask what his intentions were towards her niece!

Susan found no difficulty in leaving the house without being noticed, for her aunt and Cynthia were still in earnest colloquy in the back parlour. Fortunately, she had long since learnt from Georgiana that Beau Eversley did not live with his parents in Curzon Street, but had an establishment of his own close by in Berkeley Street. She was uncertain of the exact house, but determined to take a sedan chair, knowing she could very well rely on the chairmen to know which it was.

In a very short time, she was set down outside it. As she mounted the steps, she began to wonder for the first time exactly what she was going to say to Beau Eversley when she came face to face with him. So far, she had been concerned with the urgency of her mission, rather than its content.

It was suddenly borne in upon her that this was delicate in the extreme. Her spirit quailed, and almost she turned to run down the street again.

She shrugged despairingly, realizing that she had no choice but to go on. She raised the knocker, and tapped timidly.

The door was opened promptly by a footman in smart livery who contrived not to look surprised at her request to see his master at such an early hour of the morning. If he privately wondered a little at a young lady's coming unattended to a bachelor establishment, this also was not allowed to appear. She was invited to step inside while inquiries were made.

After a short wait, a message was brought to the effect that Mr. Eversley would see Miss Fyfield in a few moments. She was shown into a small parlour off the hall, and left alone to grapple with some very disturbed emotions.

She was still feverishly rehearsing what she would say when the door opened, making her start nervously, and Beau Eversley himself came into the room. He bowed, and glanced at the clock on the mantelpiece.

"Good morning, Miss Fyfield. I must apologize if my appearance does not do you credit, but I was obliged to scramble through my toilet in order not to keep you waiting."

She glanced at the neat folds of the cravat which appeared above the stylish brown coat he was wearing.

"You — you look perfectly all right to me," she stammered.

He gave a slight bow. "I am reassured. Naturally, I am delighted to see you; but tell me — do you usually call upon your acquaintances at such an early hour?"

"Oh, no — I beg your pardon for disturbing you," she said, in a hurried, nervous tone. "But the matter was urgent."

"Shall we sit down?" He indicated a window seat close to where she was standing, and came over to share it with her. "First of all, can I offer you some refreshment? Champagne does not agree with you, I know, but perhaps lemonade or coffee?"

She shook her head, and thanked him in a weak voice, before relapsing into a silence that lasted several minutes.

He looked at the clock again. "You mentioned an urgent matter," he prompted at last.

She started. "Yes," she admitted, unhappily. "There is something I must tell you — but I do not know how to begin!"

He looked at her thoughtfully for a moment. "Then let me hazard a guess. You are in some kind of scrape again."

She nodded, turning a pair of troubled dark eyes upon him.

"Now, what can it be this time?" he murmured, pensively.

She put up her hands to her face in a distracted gesture. "Oh, I wish I knew how to tell you!" she cried.

"I wish you did too, for it would be a great deal easier than guessing," he replied, in a soothing tone. "Can you not try? I am not such an ogre, you know. After all, I have sisters of my own, and I dare say you would be hard put to it to get into any scrape which they have not explored before you."

"Not this one!" she protested, in a muffled voice.

He sighed. "Very well, then, I must continue guessing until I hit on it." He paused. "Is it anything to do with the events of yesterday evening?"

She raised her head a little from her hands, and nodded.

"Ah!" he said, with satisfaction. "Now, let me see... Perhaps your aunt took exception to the fact that you were — how shall we put it? — a trifle elevated by your first experience of champagne? She has punished you — or threatened a punishment? And you have come to ask me to intercede for you? Is that it?"

"No — but it was something to do with the champagne, in a way —"

Her voice broke in a sob, and she hastily turned her head away. It seemed impossible to tell him.

He patted her gently on the shoulder. "My dear Susan — you don't mind if I call you Susan? You see I am treating you exactly as if you were a sister. Now pay me the same compliment, and confide in me as if I were your brother."

"But I can't!" She was trying hard now to hold back the tears. "And when you know what I have said, you will not treat me as a sister — or — or as anything at all! You will hate and — and despise me!"

"What you have said? To whom?"

"To — to my aunt—" she choked.

"And it concerns me?"

"Yes." She fumbled for a handkerchief in her reticule, and furtively wiped away the tears that were starting.

"Susan." He took her by the shoulders, and gently pulled her round to face him. "You must tell me now, without further preamble, exactly what you have said to your aunt, and why it has made you come running to me for help. Do you understand? Let us have no more evasion, but come to the point at once."

"I told her — I told her —" Her voice faltered, and died.

"Look at me, Susan." He put his hand under her chin, and forced her to look into his eyes. "What did you tell her?" he prompted.

Her cheeks burned, and she tried to evade his glance.

"I told her that — that — I was — betrothed — to you," she stammered, in a whisper.

He released her as though he had been stung. "You told her *what?*"

She repeated her words, this time in a slightly stronger tone. Now that they were out the worst hurdle was over.

He took a deep breath. "Yes," he replied thoughtfully. "I think I begin to see. The champagne must have gone to your head a little more decidedly than I had thought. And might I inquire how long we are supposed to have been engaged? Presumably I declared myself last night?"

"No — it is worse than that," said Susan, in a tone of deep mortification. "You see, it all started some weeks since, when I first came home from school to find my cousin Cynthia betrothed." As far as she could without betraying her feelings for him, she explained what had led up to the present misunderstanding. "And now they will not believe me at all!"

she finished miserably. "And what is worse, my aunt is coming to ask you for the truth!"

"I can well see that she might," he replied dryly. "It's a pity that your fantasies had to make me appear in quite such an unattractive light. I do not mind being thought capable of some things, but of inveigling a young schoolgirl into a secret engagement — no, one must draw the line somewhere! It is a great deal too bad of you, Susan."

"I know — oh, I know," she said, brokenly. "I wish with all my heart I had never said it — Miss Fanchington did warn me always to think before I spoke or acted — oh, if only I had heeded her advice!"

"As to that, advice is good or bad as the event proves. But it is no use repining. When may I expect the pleasure of a visit from your relative?"

"I should think at any minute now — that is unless she has changed her mind! But I do not think that likely, from the way she spoke."

"Then we had better decide what I am to say to her when she arrives, had we not?"

Susan stared. "What can you say, but the truth?"

"That I am not — and never was — engaged to you, secretly or otherwise?"

She nodded. "Of course."

He fixed her with a steady regard, as though he would read her inmost thoughts. "That is what you wish me to say?"

A faint colour tinged her cheeks as she nodded again.

"Very well," he said, relaxing slightly. "I have now cleared you in my own mind of a most unworthy suspicion. As you have been so open with me, perhaps I ought to confess it to you, so that you, too, can have an opportunity of hating and despising me, as you so aptly put it."

"You need not tell me, for I know what it is," interrupted Susan, the colour in her cheeks deepening. "And that is why I had to see you — I feared you might think that — that —"

"That by saying we were engaged you were deliberately trying to force me into making you an offer of marriage?" he put in, smoothly.

"Yes." She looked away from him. "That is why I felt I must come and explain things to you before my aunt arrived — so that you wouldn't think more badly of me than I deserve — though Heaven knows that is bad enough!" she concluded, choking back her sob.

He gave her another reassuring pat on the shoulder.

"Come," he said, soothingly. "It is only a schoolgirl scrape, after all. I assure you I do not regard it in a more serious light than that."

Irrationally, Susan remained uncomforted by this observation. It would have been dreadful, of course, if he had shown strong annoyance at what she had done; but to her over-sensitive feelings there was something more humiliating in his refusal to take the matter seriously. To him she was just a child, a tiresome schoolgirl who involved herself in scrapes from which at present it was his pleasure to disentangle her.

"You — you do not take me seriously at all," she said, piqued.

He cocked a quizzical eyebrow. "Should I do so?"

"I don't know." She shrugged her shoulders, trying to control a quivering lip. "It — it is scarce flattering to be treated always as a child!"

"How old are you, Susan?"

"I am seventeen — turned," she answered, with a touch of defiance.

"And I am seven and twenty," he countered, smiling, "I am old enough to be —"

"No, you are not!" Her tone was indignant. "You know very well you are not old enough to be my father!"

"I bow to your superior knowledge, of course. But that isn't what I was going to say. I was about to remind you that I could well be your elder brother. You are of the same age as Georgiana, recollect. You must forgive me if I tend to treat you somewhat in the same style."

"But — but I don't want you for a brother!" cried Susan, impetuously.

"No?" He slightly elevated his right eyebrow again, and a twinkle appeared in his eyes. This was a mannerism of his lighter moments which Susan found progressively endearing. "Then what do you want me as? Your betrothed, perhaps?"

Possibly he had forgotten for a moment the secret which his sister had confided to him. Perhaps it was devilment, perhaps some other reason which he himself did not quite understand. Whatever prompted the mocking question, it had the effect of plunging Susan into deep embarrassment.

"I — I wish you will not tease me — please!" she implored, between blushes. "I know it was wicked of me to say what I did — and — and most improper — but I did not mean it to be so — at the time, I just said the first thing that came into my head! I did not think!"

"Why myself more than another, though?" he persisted.

"Because — oh, because you were the only one who danced with me, I suppose! And — and you are Beau Eversley, after all — it means something to be engaged to you!"

He bowed ironically. "I don't think I have ever met anyone with so happy a knack of depressing all one's most cherished pretensions," he said, reflectively. "I could not but be aware that I had established some small reputation in the world — of what value, I leave you to be the judge. But I had dared to hope that the lady who would one day do me the honour to be my wife might be activated by other motives than those of a mere seeking after — shall we say notoriety? I feel that the word 'fame' would scarcely be appropriate, in this case."

"Oh, you do not understand at all!" cried Susan, distressed. "I know you are in part funning me, but underneath you're part in earnest; and I cannot bear you to think that — that —"

She stopped, unable to put her tangled emotions readily into words.

He waited a moment, watching her face, which betrayed more than she realized of what was passing in her mind.

"What can't you bear me to think?" he prompted, gently.

"That I'm the kind of girl who likes to have something — anything — to boast about! Just as my cousin accused me of hating the thought of her being betrothed while I myself am not! It isn't like that at all!" She broke off, shaking her head in a puzzled, frustrated gesture, and then continued, "And yet, in a way, it is... Oh, how can I make you understand when I don't even understand myself?"

"You might try," he suggested, very quietly, "by simply telling me your thoughts just as they come into your mind, and leaving me to make what sense I can of them."

She nodded, and gave him a shy, grateful look.

"You are much kinder than I ever realized, and so — so understanding!" She hesitated for a moment, then went on, in a low tone, "Cynthia thought I was jealous of her because she was betrothed. I wasn't a bit, of that, not really — but it was just one more thing that she had, and I had not. You see —" she burst out, in a sudden access of self-realization — "I think I always have been a little bit jealous of Cynthia!"

He nodded. "I dare say Mrs. Fyfield would naturally show a certain partiality for her own child."

"In a way — but yet it's not really that," replied Susan, slowly. "Aunt Hattie's always been just, when Cynthia and I quarrelled, and she's been kind to me in her detached way. Of course, I was only home in the holidays, you know, and I went to Miss Fanchington's Seminary when I was seven years old. But I'm jealous of Cynthia because — oh, because it's *her* home, and her *Mama*, while I —" a world of sorrow was suddenly mirrored in the dark eyes she turned towards him — "I haven't got anything that is truly mine. Sometimes, I have wanted so much — to have someone of my very own, to — to love me, and hold me in regard high above all others — I can't even remember my own parents, you see —"

She turned her head away from him abruptly.

"So I think that is the real reason," she finished, in a muffled voice, "why I suddenly wanted to pretend that at last I did possess someone of my very own — and someone I could boast of possessing, too — someone whom others would envy me for having!"

The Fashionable World might have been hard put to it at that moment to recognize its leader, Beau Eversley. The fine hazel eyes which normally would hold either a twinkle or a mocking light, were now deepened by compassion. Like many another, he possessed qualities which were rarely called into being in the gay, easy, frivolous life that he led. But when he spoke, he did not betray what he was feeling.

"I collect your parents died when you were very young?"

The calm, matter-of-fact tone soothed her as no expression of sympathy could have done at that particular moment.

"I was not quite two years old. My father was Uncle Ralph's younger brother — Uncle Ralph was Aunt Hattie's husband, you know." He nodded. "My father was a naval officer, and contracted a fever in some foreign port. He died on the homeward voyage, and the shock killed my mother, who was — in a delicate condition, for she was shortly expecting a second child."

"I see. And so your father's brother took you in."

Susan shook her head. "No. It was Aunt Hattie, for Uncle Ralph died soon after Cynthia was born. I never knew him."

He raised his brows. "Strange, surely, that your aunt by marriage should offer you a home? Were there no relatives on your mother's side to come forward?"

"I never heard of any. I sometimes used to ask my aunt about that, but she had nothing to tell me. I can only suppose that, if there were any, they did not wish to take me. And I don't wonder," she finished, despondently, "for they must have guessed how I would turn out! I suppose now even Aunt Hattie may be trying to find someone to take me off her hands — though who would do so is more than I can imagine!"

"May I make a suggestion?" His voice was cool and amused. "What would you say to — myself?"

Chapter VIII: A Telling Point

For a moment Susan stared at Beau Eversley as though he had lost his wits.

"You are making game of me!" she exclaimed, at last, in a voice trembling with indignation.

"Not the least little bit in the world," he answered, soothingly. "It occurs to me that a very good way out of this situation for you — if you would not object to it, that is — would be for us to tell your aunt that we are indeed betrothed."

"But — but," stammered Susan, hardly knowing what she was saying, "but — it isn't true!"

"Then we must make it true," he said, smiling at her bewilderment. "Come, what do you say? Should you object to having me for your affianced husband?"

She could not speak; but for a brief moment her eyes held all that was in her heart. He drew in his breath sharply, and looked away.

"You do not need to give the matter such earnest consideration," he continued, still in the same light tone. "The engagement would be only of a short duration. You would be at liberty to end it whenever you pleased."

"I — I don't quite understand —" Painfully she groped for words, her mind spinning.

"Let me explain. You feel that your aunt may perhaps adopt stern measures with you over this little affair; and whether she does or not, there will be your cousin ready to crow over you when she learns the truth." He saw Susan wince slightly, and felt encouraged to continue. "But if we were to say that you were telling the truth all the time, and that there really was — is

— an engagement between us, then their guns would be successfully spiked."

"But — you do not — cannot — wish to become engaged to me!"

"You are more than common modest," he said, with a twinkle in his eye. "You must know that you are a very attractive young lady."

She was very still for a moment. "Do you — do you really think so?" she breathed.

"Undoubtedly." He bent over her and lifted one of the ringlets that lay on her neck. "Glossy black hair, an elfin face, and a pair of fine, dark eyes — what more could anyone desire?"

She sprang to her feet, turning her face away from him.

"But you do not — care for me — in that way," she said, hurriedly. "So why are you willing to do this for me?"

He hesitated for a moment. The truth was altogether too complex for him completely to understand, let alone explain.

"Let us say that I feel impelled to assist a lady in distress — especially when the assistance involves so small a sacrifice on my part."

"'It is not a small thing to become engaged!"

He rose to his feet. "Not in the normal way, of course," he agreed; smoothly. "But this would be only a temporary arrangement, to be ended at your whim. We could still keep it secret from the world at large — only your aunt and cousin need know of it We could tell them that we did not intend to make any formal announcement until your eighteenth birthday."

"Oh!" She swung round to face him, her eyes dancing. "Oh, that would be famous!"

"Yes," he agreed, complacently. "I rather thought so, myself. I take it that your birthday is not imminent?"

"Oh, no! Not for ages — almost a year!" she confessed.

"So that gives us plenty of time. In a month or two, you can break off the betrothal."

Her face sobered again. "Yes," she said, slowly. "I see. But what excuse can we make for breaking it off? Will it not cause a deal of unpleasant gossip?"

He shook his head. "Without a formal announcement, none need know of it. And in any case no gossip can possibly attach to you, my dear, for you will be the one to put an end to the affair. My conduct will offend you in some way — most likely in the obvious way." He broke off, and laughed lightly. "Oh, yes," he finished, cynically. "I can see no difficulty at all about that part of the business."

"But suppose —" began Susan, then stopped, colouring.

"Suppose what?"

"Oh, nothing."

There was a short silence, then he said: "So we are agreed? In that case —"

He was interrupted by a tap on the door. In response to his invitation, a footman entered to announce that a lady had called to see Mr. Eversley.

"Admit her," directed the Beau, and turned to Susan with a smile. "I fancy we know who it is."

The man hesitated for a second, looked doubtfully at Susan, then withdrew to do his master's bidding.

"Oh, dear!" whispered Susan, nervously. "Do — do you think we can really persuade her to believe us?" He took her hand, which was trembling slightly, and patted it reassuringly.

"Courage!" he said, raising his eyebrow in the way she liked. "The day is ours, you may depend!"

The door opened, and a lady entered the room.

They both stared. It was certainly not the lady they had expected. She was dark and slim, and was dressed in a smart riding habit of golden brown, with a saucy little hat perched on the side of her head.

She stood still for a moment, coolly taking in the scene before her, then sank into a curtsy that was a masterpiece of irony. If any woman in London knew how to convey so much in a gesture, it was Maria McCann.

"Well," she said, in an amused tone. "Your servant appears to have blundered. It is plain that I am interrupting a charming tête-à-tête, and I will remove myself instantly. Nay, never blush, madam —" addressing herself to Susan, who had hastily withdrawn her hand from Beau Eversley's, and was looking confused — "the fault is mine, for bursting in upon you in so unceremonious a fashion. My excuse must be that I had thought to find the gentleman alone." Her expressive eyes fixed themselves on the Beau reproachfully. "We had an engagement for this morning which has doubtless slipped his memory." She shrugged, and smiled. "No matter. It is not of the least consequence — no, not at all."

Hugh Eversley recovered himself. "Wait here for me," he said to Susan in a low tone. "I shall return presently and then I'll escort you home." He stepped forward with a ceremonious bow. "Madam," he addressed the actress, "if you will please step outside with me, I fancy I can give you an explanation. There has been a sudden, unavoidable change in my plans."

Maria McCann laughed in a studied, melodic trill. "Sure, and I'll be bound there has!" she cried, at her most Irish. "And who would be after blaming you, at all? Not myself, and there's the truth on't!" She paused, and eyed Susan from top to toe. "But will you not present me to your fair charmer?" she finished.

"Sure, and it's cradle snatching you are, Mr. Eversley, for this sweet babe should still be nestling under the shelter of her Mama's wing!"

Before the Beau could reply to this, Susan herself broke in, her voice warm with indignation.

"Since you ask it, my name is Susan Fyfield. And even if I had a Mama to shield me, I should not need her protection, I thank you, for I am very well able to take care of myself! I do not need to be presented to you, for I know quite well who you are — you are Mistress Maria McCann, from the playhouse."

The actress inclined her head gracefully. "And so I am. Aren't you the clever one, knowing that? So you have no Mama? Then let me warn you, Miss Fyfield —" she wagged an admonitory finger on which a large diamond flashed — "against fascinating gentlemen such as Mr. Eversley here."

At this point, the fascinating gentleman in question took hold of Maria McCann's nicely rounded arm and began to urge her gently but insistently towards the door.

"There is no occasion to warn me against anyone!" exclaimed Susan, with flashing eyes. "I am quite able to judge for myself who is — or is not — to be trusted!"

"That would provide a very good exit line, my dear," replied Mistress McCann, as she moved out of the room at Beau Eversley's side. "Undoubtedly, you have the flair — you, too, might have made an actress."

At this point, the Beau strategically closed the door upon Susan, and guided his companion into an adjoining room.

"I suppose I ought to begin by begging your pardon for being late for our appointment," he said, ruefully.

"Don't be after doing anything that goes against the grain, now!" she answered, laughing. "It is, of course, unpardonable of you to keep me waiting, and it will be long enough before you'll be having the opportunity for such a thing again —"

"You are as adept at taking me up wrongly as that child out there," he said, with a wry smile, inclining his head in the direction of the room where they had left Susan. "But the plain truth is this — the girl is a friend of my young sister's; and, finding herself in a bit of a scrape, she came to me for help."

She cocked her head on one side, and gave him a knowing look. "Now what kind of scrape would a young girl of that quality be in that would need her coming to a gentleman for help, at all?"

"I am not at liberty to discuss that," he said, stiffly. "It is a private matter."

She nodded briefly, and glanced at the clock. "Of course: it would be. And now I must go. I have other appointments to keep, though you may not realize it." He put out a hand to detain her. "I am sorry about today," he said, with a regretful smile that was full of charm. "Will you ride with me tomorrow morning, instead?"

Her answering smile showed no rancour, but her reply was as firm as it was prompt. "I will not. Indeed, you can't expect that I should."

"Expect, no. Hope, yes. It is, I realize, more than I deserve —"

"Much more. And certainly more than you will be after receiving. And now, if you will forgive me —"

He put his hand on her arm. "I am the one in need of forgiveness. Say you'll relent?"

She tapped his hand with the riding crop which she was carrying. "Perhaps. Some day." Her voice was careless. She paused for a moment, regarding him steadily with her deep blue eyes. "Have a care to that child," she said, suddenly, in a different tone. "She's young, and it is clear that she —" She broke off. "No matter for that. But I was young myself — once — and I understand."

"I'll see you out," he replied.

He accompanied her to the street, where a groom was waiting with her horse. She nodded a careless farewell as she swung lightly into the saddle, and rode away. He stood for a moment looking after her thoughtfully before he re-entered the house.

He found Susan standing by the window. She turned with a guilty start as he entered the room.

"Has she gone?" she asked, shyly. "I — I am sorry if I caused any unpleasantness —"

"Don't trouble your head over that," he replied, briefly. "Naturally, both of us assumed that the visitor would be your aunt. However, since Mrs. Fyfield has not yet called on me, we must go to her."

He pulled the bell, and ordered his coach to be sent round immediately. Susan scarcely had time to settle herself into the luxurious red leather interior before she was alighting outside her aunt's house in Duke Street.

When they were admitted by Mrs. Fyfield's shabby footman, Susan could not help for a moment contrasting her own home with Beau Eversley's elegant establishment. The next minute, every consideration of this kind gave way before her mingled apprehension and excitement. She led the way to the parlour where she had left her aunt and cousin — could it be possible? — barely an hour ago.

She opened the door, and found both ladies within. They appeared to be on the point of going out, for they were both dressed for the street.

"Great heavens! Susan!" exclaimed Mrs. Fyfield, while Cynthia contented herself with a small shriek of surprise. "Where on earth have you been, child? I declare, the most melancholy suppositions have been engaging your poor cousin and myself — oh!" She stopped on seeing Beau Eversley step into the room. "So you are not alone! Oh, Lud bless me! I declare I don't know what to think!"

The Beau took charge at this point, and, making a very handsome leg, wished the ladies good morning. They replied automatically to his civilities, but looked almost as awkward and embarrassed as Susan herself. He saw that he was not to have much help in the business, but this did not disturb him in the least. His puckish sense of humour gave him a certain enjoyment of what to many would have seemed an awkward situation.

"I have come, madam," he began to Mrs. Fyfield, "to explain myself. Alas, I fear you may feel that an explanation is long overdue."

As he added the last remark in a penitent tone, he glanced slyly at Susan. He had the satisfaction of seeing some of the embarrassment ease from her expression, and a subdued twinkle appear in her dark eyes.

"Oh, no!" exclaimed Mrs. Fyfield, agitated. "That is to say, yes — if what Susan has been telling me is in any way the truth — but, of course, it couldn't be! I do declare," she breathed, looking around her in evident confusion, "that I must be dreaming! This can't be happening — I shall wake up presently — most likely something I ate last night has disagreed with me —"

"I assure you, ma'am," put in the Beau, smoothly, "that only the very best caterers were responsible for the supper which was offered to my sister's guests."

"Oh, dear me, yes, of course — to be sure!" protested Susan's aunt. "I did not mean to suggest that there was anything *wrong* with the food — everything was of the most sumptuous of course —"

Beau Eversley bowed. "You reassure me, Mrs. Fyfield."

"What Mama means," put in Cynthia, who was recovering her composure a little, "is that this all seems like some dreadful nightmare."

The Beau raised an eyebrow. "Dear me, do you really feel it is as bad as that?" he asked, trying to keep a laugh out of his voice. "I am to take it, then, what you do not approve of me as a suitor for Miss Susan?"

Cynthia turned an unlovely shade of red, while Mrs. Fyfield gaped at him for a moment. Suddenly the power of speech returned to her.

"So there *is* an engagement, after all, and Susan was not making it up!" she cried. "Lud, and I was sure the child was at her old games again — she has always had the most powerful imagination! You can have no idea!" She broke off, and stared at Beau Eversley in a puzzled way. "But I cannot at all understand it," she went on, in a quieter tone. "How could you become sufficiently acquainted with Susan while she was at Miss Fanchington's Seminary for a betrothal to take place? And what could you find to attract you in a young schoolroom miss when you might have had your pick of the Town's belles? And why," she finished, shrewdly, "should the matter be contrived in so secret a fashion? — you will forgive me, I am sure, but I had almost used the word 'underhand'."

The amusement died out of Hugh Eversley's face for a moment.

"You have a right to feel as you do, Mrs. Fyfield, and I have much to be forgiven in this affair." Susan opened her mouth to protest, for this was more than she could swallow; but he made a slight gesture of warning, and she subsided.

"My sister Georgiana managed to contrive meetings between your niece and myself," he continued glibly. "It was most improper of me, I own —"

"And most improper of Susan, too!" exclaimed Cynthia, with a snap. "She must have been totally lost to all that is maidenly and virtuous!"

He turned a steely eye upon her. "You may say what you choose of my conduct, madam; but may I remind you that in maligning Miss Susan you are speaking of my future wife?"

Susan drew in her breath sharply.

"And my I remind you, Mr. Eversley, that she is my cousin, and has been for many a long year, before ever you set eyes on her?" retorted Cynthia, who for the moment had allowed her jealousy of Susan's betrothal to overcome her reverence for the noted Beau Eversley. "No virtuous girl would consent for one moment to a secret engagement — it is only one degree less bad than an out-and-out elopement, let me tell you!"

"I'm afraid she is quite right, you know," said Mrs. Fyfield, more reasonably. "It was not at all the thing, and if only you were not so wildly impetuous, Susan, and so hopelessly romantical, you could never have brought yourself to agree to such an improper arrangement!"

The quick colour started to Susan's cheeks, and her eyes dropped away before Hugh Eversley's reassuring glance.

"The blame's all mine," he said. "Knowing your niece as you do, you will not need me to tell you that her innocence was too profound for her ever to have realized the impropriety of a secret engagement. I alone knew that I was acting wrongly — though, at the time, in a view of her extreme youth, it seemed best not to press the matter further. However," he went on, in a brisker tone, "I am here now to put things right, and to ask for your niece's hand in due form. Apart from the irregularity of our previous betrothal, is there any reason that you know of, madam, why I may not now have your consent to pay my addresses to Miss Susan in the conventional manner?"

A change came over Mrs. Fyfield's face, where a number of conflicting expressions had been striving for mastery throughout this speech.

"Oh, Lud!" she said, shaking her head in bewilderment. "Lud save us. I don't know what to say, and that's the truth on't!"

"You mean you need time to think over my application for your niece's hand?"

She shook her head. "I mean I don't know what to do! I am not at all sure — that is to say, perhaps you ought —"

She broke off, pausing a moment while the others stared at her in uncomprehending silence. Then she appeared to make up her mind.

"It's no good — I see I must tell you, after all, in spite of my undertaking never to do so. But circumstances alter cases, and this was not foreseen — though it should have been, come to that, for girls who will grow up, and suitors will come for them —"

"Mama!" interrupted Cynthia, sharply. "What is it you're trying to say? For heaven's sake, come to the point!"

Mrs. Fyfield looked round at the mystified faces before her, and drew a deep breath.

"Yes, I must come to the point." She turned to Hugh Eversley. "And the point is, Mr. Eversley, that it's of no use your applying to me for Susan's hand. In truth I don't know to whom you should apply, unless it might be to her lawyer."

A puzzled frown appeared on Beau Eversley's face. "Her lawyer? But surely, as she is in your care, and you are her aunt —"

Mrs. Fyfield shook her head. "That's just it. I am not. Susan is not my niece — she is not related to me at all. In fact," she concluded, in the tone of one who has failed to give satisfaction, "I have no notion who she may be. All I know about her with any certainty is that she has a considerable fortune at her disposal."

Chapter IX: The Waif

Nobody moved or spoke for a few moments. Then Susan flung herself forward.

"Aunt Hattie, what in the world are you saying? Of course I am your niece — my father was your husband's brother, and he left me in your care — you told me so ages and ages ago, I well remember it —"

"I am sorry, child, but it was all the completest fabrication. Of course, I know one should never tell lies to children; but what was I to tell you? Like this business of your engagement, there were so many situations for which I had no guidance — the circumstances were most unusual, you see —"

"This is absurd, Mama!" exclaimed Cynthia, recovering speech. "I know very well that my father's brother Roger died on the high seas, for you have told me of it many times. And that he left a young widow somewhere in Dorset, who soon afterwards died in childbed. And Susan —"

"That part of the story was true," admitted Mrs. Fyfield, with a trace of artistic pride in her manner. "It seemed to me that if I had to pass Susan off as a relation — and this was required of me — I could not do better than provide her with your poor Uncle Roger and his wife as parents. Dorset is a long way off, and your poor Papa had no relatives left alive nowadays who would be at all fit to make the journey to London, so I felt safe from exposure there. And it is always easier to deceive people if you are telling them part, at any rate, of the truth. Not that," she concluded, hastily, "I would recommend either of you girls to deceive anyone; for apart from being very wrong and wicked it is also vastly uncomfortable, as I can tell you from my own experience —"

"So I am not your niece," said Susan, slowly, breaking in on these moral reflections, "I am not related to you at all?"

Mrs. Fyfield shook her head. "Not in consanguinity. But that does not alter the fact that I am very fond of you, child — I should not at all mind if you were truly my niece. Indeed, I have been thinking of you as related to me for these many years past."

"But why?" asked Susan, looking completely lost. "Why did you have to pretend that I was related to you? Who was it who asked you to do it, and why?"

"Yes, Mama," echoed Cynthia. "I think you owe us all an explanation — perhaps even —" with an acid glance at the Beau — "perhaps even Mr. Eversley. After all, he will want to know just who it is he has got himself betrothed to. You had better tell us the whole, without further delay."

So far Hugh Eversley had remained silent, watching each one intently, and listening closely to all that passed. Now he addressed Mrs. Fyfield for the first time since she had made her startling revelation.

"Perhaps you would like me to leave, ma'am. You may not care to speak in the presence of an outsider."

"You are scarce an outsider, sir, since you are betrothed to my — to Susan," amended Mrs. Fyfield, hurriedly. "No, it is better that you stay, for then perhaps you will understand what ought to be done — which is more than I can tell, for I cannot think whom you should approach to ask for her hand, as I said before. It must be the lawyer — yes, assuredly Mr. Watson is the man, you may depend on it."

Beau Eversley hesitated. The whole affair was rapidly taking on a very different complexion. Drawn on partly by compassion and partly by other motives which he had not yet had time to analyse, he had offered to pretend that Susan's story was true. The pretence would have served well enough for Mrs. Fyfield and even for her shrewish daughter; but a man — and, moreover, a lawyer — was altogether another matter. If the girl had been left in his charge, this Mr. Watson would naturally wish to see her betrothal arranged in a proper manner. There would be talk of settlements, and it might be difficult to persuade him that a formal announcement ought not to be made. And a formal announcement would bring undesirable complications to the inevitable breaking of the betrothal. The least desirable of these complications, in Beau Eversley's view, would be the gossip that would surround Susan.

Fortunately, his hesitation was scarcely noticed. Both Susan and Cynthia were intent on hearing a full explanation from Mrs. Fyfield. After several promptings and false starts, they did eventually manage to glean the story from her.

"I was in such dire straits after your Papa died," she began, addressing herself at first to Cynthia. "I have told you often how we were left —" Cynthia assented hastily, trying to avoid a wealth of unnecessary detail — "so I will not weary you with that again. The question was, what could I do to mend my fortunes? Our fortunes, I should say, for though you were at that time only a babe I had to look to the future. There were no wealthy relatives to whom I might apply for help, so I began to cast about for some way of making money. At one time I even—" she hesitated for a moment — "I even considered keeping a gaming house."

Cynthia exclaimed in horror.

"Oh, it would have been very select, you know," Mrs. Fyfield said, hastily. "But, however, in the end I could not think that it was quite the thing for a gentlewoman, however impoverished, so I abandoned the idea."

"I should think so, indeed," said Cynthia, impatiently. "But do, pray, come to the point, Mama!"

"Very well, child, I am coming to it, only I must explain how things were. Well, then I saw the advertisement."

"What advertisement?" asked Susan, who was hanging anxiously on every word.

"It was in one of the journals — I forget which," replied Mrs. Fyfield. "But it doesn't signify. It asked for a lady of breeding who would be willing to receive a young child into her family in return for a handsome remuneration. It gave Mr. Watson's address in Chancery Lane. I didn't give it serious consideration, at first, you know; but I was ready to clutch at straws, and so I wrote off immediately, never thinking to hear any more."

"But you did hear," stated Susan.

Mrs. Fyfield nodded. "Yes. Within a few days, Mr. Watson himself waited on me. "I suppose," she said, thoughtfully, "he came to look at the house, and see if he thought it a suitable home for the child — but I never thought of that until now. Anyway, he asked a deal of questions. I began to find it all very tiresome, and to regret having ever answered the stupid advertisement — until he mentioned the remuneration. And then, of course, I saw at once that it was the very thing I had been looking for. But I didn't wish to appear too eager, so I began to ask questions in my turn. He had already told me that the child was a girl of between two and three years old. I asked him about her parentage, and why a foster home was being sought for her; but I might have saved my breath. He refused to tell me anything beyond that her name was Susan and that she was a normal, healthy child."

"So at least my Christian name is my own," said Susan, in a small voice.

Beau Eversley glanced quickly at her. For some time now, his gaze had been fixed on Mrs. Fyfield as he followed the story she had to tell. He saw at once that the expression on Susan's face had changed. At first, it had been one of simple bewilderment; now it showed unhappiness as well. She looked what she had been all those years ago — a waif in need of a safe shelter. He felt the stirrings of compassion.

"As to that, you need not worry, child, for until this affair of your betrothal I declare I had been thinking of you for many years as a Fyfield, and my niece too. Even if I were to discover now, at last, what your real parentage is, I doubt if I could alter my way of thinking. Indeed," she added, patting Susan's hand in a kindly way, "I don't wish to; for, with all your rash ways, you're a good girl, by and large, and I'm very fond of you."

"Thank you," said Susan, in a barely audible voice.

"So you were paid for giving Susan a home," put in Cynthia, bluntly. "And what about her board and lodging, clothes and school fees, and all the rest?"

"Oh, if you must have every little detail," retorted her mother, "I submitted all bills on her behalf to the lawyer for payment. If there happened to be anything a little bit out of the way, I would go and see him and explain all about it. He always made generous provision for her needs — most generous."

"I suppose," said Cynthia, thoughtfully, "that she doesn't happen to be this lawyer's child?"

"Oh, no, I cannot think it!" cried Mrs. Fyfield. "He's not a wealthy man, and Susan has a considerable fortune at her disposal."

"How do you know that?"

"Why, he often told me so, and also that he has the sole administration of it."

"She might have been left the money by a relative. It does not necessarily have to come from her father."

"But it would be such a strange way for Mr. Watson to behave, Cynthia! Surely no man would board his own daughter out while he had a home of his own to which he might take her!"

"May I ask if you know anything of this lawyer's domestic arrangements, ma'am?" asked Hugh Eversley.

"Why, very little, for no one could call Mr. Watson a chatty kind of man. But I collect that he has a wife and several children of both sexes, so there can be no likelihood of his being Susan's father."

"You can't be sure of that," said Cynthia. "There might be circumstances —"

"Oh, stop it, all of you!" cried Susan, suddenly, burying her face in her hands. "I don't think I can stand any more!"

Beau Eversley took a step towards her, then checked. Mrs. Fyfield went to her side, and placed an aim about her.

"There, there, my love!" She turned to the Beau. "I think perhaps you should go now, Mr. Eversley, and come back tomorrow, when we can decide what is to be done. It has all been a dreadful shock for the poor child, I am sure, and no one can wonder if she is quite overset by it. I will get her to lie down for a little, and perhaps she will feel better presently."

"You are right, ma'am. Miss Susan has certainly sustained enough emotional upset for one day, and she will do well to rest quietly for a while. You must long have been wishing me absent, so I will take myself off now, and wait upon you tomorrow, as you suggest. Can you name a convenient hour?"

"No!" exclaimed Susan, in a muffled voice. "No, do not come tomorrow!"

He paused in the act of making a cold bow to Cynthia. "You do not wish me to come?"

"Not that — not exactly!" Her voice broke on a sob. "It is just that — you cannot wish to — anyway, it was all —"

She broke off, evidently trying hard to fight back the tears.

"No one can possibly want to — to become engaged to a — a nameless female — so we had better break it off!"

"But, my love!" protested Mrs. Fyfield. "There's no need to take it so hard! I dare say that Mr. Watson will be very ready to divulge the secret of your parentage to your affianced husband, even though he would not entrust it to me. After all, women do talk, I know — one must admit it — and there must have been some particular reason why the truth should not be spread abroad —"

"Yes, indeed, Mama," interrupted Cynthia, tartly. "There must have been some particular reason. What does it seem to you that reason can be?"

A long silence greeted these words. Then Susan spoke, hiding her face on Mrs. Fyfield's shoulder.

"I know what she means — and I dare say she's right. So that's all done with now — you — you won't need to come again, sir — goodbye —"

Her voice tailed off.

"On the contrary," said Beau Eversley, firmly. "I shall wait on Mrs. Fyfield tomorrow morning at — shall we say noon, ma'am? And after that, I intend to see your lawyer, Miss Susan."

Chapter X: Masquerade

That same evening, Beau Eversley arrived at his parents' home to escort his sister Georgiana to a masquerade given by the Radleys, who were old friends of the Eversley family.

"And you may count yourself fortunate," he reminded Georgy, "for if either your Mama or Evelina had been able to accompany you, I should have cried off. Masquerades are not in my line."

"Not even when it is a masquerade at the Radleys' house?" she teased him. "Dearest Hugh, you do say the drollest things! But how do I look?" She pirouetted so that her aquamarine silk domino billowed around her. "Tell me, do you think anyone will recognize me in this?"

She fastened a black loo mask over her face.

He surveyed her quizzically. "A domino and mask is an effective disguise for most people, but you've reckoned without the Eversley hair."

"But if I pull my hood on — so?" She suited the action to the word.

"Ah, then you might pass unrecognized. But why should you wish to do so?"

"Silly, it's a masquerade, and there's no fun if everyone knows me at once."

"I wonder you do not think a mere domino and mask too tame a disguise. I expected to find you garbed as a classical deity, or some historical character."

Georgy pouted. "I did have some costumes sent round for me to choose from, and I fancied myself strongly as an Eastern Sultana, but Mama and Evelina thought it was not quite the thing. So after that, I could not like any of the others, and I sent them all back to the costumiers, and ordered this, instead — Eve thought it quite becoming — and I do think the colour does something to my eyes, don't you, Hugh?"

"Don't regard that, my dear," he said, teasingly. "I dare say you'll escape notice altogether in the inevitable crush. But did you say Eve was still here with you? I thought she was going down to Richmond to stay with the children while Cunningham was obliged to be out of Town on business?"

"So she is, but she doesn't go until tomorrow. I must say I wonder at her being content to shut herself away in the country while there is so much entertainment to be had here in Town."

"It doesn't occur to you that she may not enjoy the diversions of Town without her husband to share them? Or even that she may wish to be with their children again?"

"But she sees the children frequently — and as for needing a husband to share one's amusements, pooh! That is old-fashioned, let me tell you! When I am married, I mean to go my own way; and my husband may do as he pleases, so long as he doesn't interfere with me too much, or expect me to be always with him — which would be vastly tedious, besides being quite out of fashion!"

"It is always instructive to listen to your notions," replied her brother, dryly. "If only your prospective suitors could know the half, you'd be a spinster for life, I assure you." He broke off to signal to a footman to bring the black domino which he had laid aside on entering the house. "As it is, my dear Georgy, I fear they will be sadly taken in by the alluring exterior of what I can only describe as a baggage. Are you ready to go?"

They were almost the last to arrive at the masquerade. As Beau Eversley had predicted, they found the ballroom crowded with a gay throng in colourful costume. Barbara Radley came forward with her brother Peter to greet them. In a softly draped white gown in the Classical mode, with her flaxen curls bound high on her head with bands of gold ribbon, she might surely have rivalled that long dead Helen whom she was impersonating.

Peter Radley, who was a close friend of the Beau's, soon bore Georgiana away to dance.

"Will you honour me?" Hugh asked Barbara, with his careless smile.

She hesitated for a moment, then accepted his arm.

"I fear it's a sad crush," she apologized. "Mama believes that some uninvited guests may have slipped in, for we tried to keep numbers down to what would be comfortable."

"Don't mind that," he replied, smiling down into her blue eyes. "Tomorrow it will be all over Town that the Radley's masquerade was a shocking squeeze — a sure sign of success."

"I suppose you are right," she acknowledged, with a shy smile.

She was silent for a while, and Beau Eversley eyed her reflectively. Lovely as she was, why was it that she no longer had any power over him? There had been a time, not long since, when a look from those blue eyes, the lightest touch of her hand, could intoxicate his senses. Like all his infatuations — and he had known many — the enchantment had lasted briefly, then faded abruptly. But under its influence, he admitted to himself, for the first time he had seriously contemplated matrimony. Before he had committed himself, however, the spell had vanished completely, and he no longer cared for her. He knew that he had aroused some expectations and that she had been hurt, though perhaps not as deeply as Viscountess Eversley chose to make out. His mother's opinions on the subject were, he well knew, coloured by the belief that it was high time her eldest son was married, and the knowledge that there could scarcely be a more suitable match for him.

The dance ended, and Barbara's hand for the succeeding one was hastily claimed by a dark, stocky young man called Warburton, who had been anxiously watching Barbara and her present partner for some time. Hugh turned away, with a cynical smile. If Barbara had lost one admirer, she had certainly gained another, he reflected.

He glanced around him, but saw no one else at the moment with whom he had the least desire to dance. The ballroom was very hot, and he noticed that some long doors at the far side of the room had been set open, revealing glimpses of the terrace and the garden beyond. He began to elbow his way discreetly across the room, and presently stepped out on to the terrace, gratefully inhaling the fresh air.

The June night was warm and mellow, and the scent of roses floated to his nostrils. He thought he would stroll in the garden for a while, and started to move forward towards the steps which led down to it.

As he did so, he caught sight of a flutter of draperies behind some ornamental dwarf trees which stood at the side of the terrace. It suddenly occurred to him that someone had been standing out here looking into the ballroom, and that his appearance had caused the observer to seek concealment. Why? And who was it, man or woman?

With a sudden, quick movement, he turned towards the trees.

He heard a stifled gasp, and at once a shadowy figure dashed from cover, racing down the steps and starting along a path which wound its way through the garden amid shrubs and trees.

Although he had recognized the fugitive for a female from the moment she started to run, it did not deter him from giving chase. He was curious to know who she might be, and why she had been watching from the terrace. Besides, if she chose to behave in so unconventional a way, he considered her fair enough game.

There could be no doubt of the outcome of the chase. He easily caught her up, and reached out to grasp her. Alarmed, she tried to move out of his way, and almost stumbled over a loose stone. He caught her in his arms to save her from falling. She struggled to free herself; and, as she did so, some movement of her head struck a chord of familiarity in him. "Maria McCann!" he exclaimed, surprised. "Now, b'God, I believe it's none other!"

He jerked her round to face him, drawing her as close as the voluminous folds of her domino would permit. There was no moon, and her face was almost completely covered by a black lace mask; but he could see her eyes behind it, glittering with some emotion — whether of love, fear or hate, he could not tell.

"I can't guess what you're doing here," he said, softly, "but you'll find you won't escape without paying forfeit."

He pressed his mouth ruthlessly on hers.

For a moment, she yielded, motionless; then a strangled sob escaped her as he released her abruptly.

"You're not Maria — then who the devil? —"

She tore herself from his slackened grasp, and turning, fled into the night.

He stood looking after her, a puzzled frown on his face. Then, with a careless shrug, he retraced his steps to the house.

When he reached the terrace, he found Peter Radley waiting there for him.

"I trust I don't interrupt an assignation?" asked Peter, with exaggerated politeness. "Am I mistaken, or did I see you with a female in the garden?"

"Been taking a breather, that's all," replied Hugh, carelessly. "I suppose you didn't happen to notice Georgy, at all, on your way through the ballroom? I promised mother to give an eye to her, you know what a madcap she is."

"If I'm not much mistaken, she'll be kept busy all the evening dancing with her admirers. When last I set eyes on her, three or four of 'em were lined up awaiting their turn to lead her on to the floor, and eyeing each other like so many battling tomcats. She's a rage already — I remember it was the same with your sister Evelina, before she married Cunningham. The irresistible Eversleys what?"

"I notice young Warburton's dangling after *your* sister," countered Hugh, smiling.

"Yes." Peter shot a quick, sidelong glance at his friend. "D'you mind, Hugh?"

The Beau lifted an eyebrow. "Did you suppose I might?"

"Oh, not at all!" replied Peter, hurriedly. "But there was a time — however, never mind that. Yes, my mother feels that Warburton may soon declare himself."

"Would he be acceptable?"

"Oh, yes — to us, that is. But of course, the real question is, would he be acceptable to my grandfather? I tell you straight, Hugh, if I had to apply to that old devil for any girl's hand she'd remain a spinster, whatever her charms!"

Hugh nodded. "I collect Sir Josiah Radley is a trifle — ah — Gothic, shall we say?"

"Understating the case," replied Peter, emphatically. "A regular Tartar, I can tell you! Thank the Lord he don't often summon us to his presence, for there's not one of us don't quake in our shoes, when he does!"

"Gout?" asked the Beau. "Or apoplexy?"

"Sheer bad temper, if you ask me! I collect there was some kind of fuss over my Uncle Robert, at one time, and he's been cross-grained ever since. Damn silly, too, because all that happened years ago, and there's no profit in turning over old bones, is there? But for the Lord's sake don't let's talk about *him* — damn distasteful subject at a party, or anywhere else, for that matter! I came to see if you'd care to sample the champagne punch before word of its excellence gets round. Then I thought we might slip into the cardroom until supper time — that's if I can elude the maternal eye for as long as that, of course!"

In the ballroom, a dance had just ended, and Georgiana was being escorted back to her seat against the wall by a young man who was doing his utmost to make a good impression on her. The floor was crowded, so that it was impossible to walk across it without being jostled from time to time. This was why Georgy did not at first heed a gentle touch on her arm, and only turned sharply when she felt what amounted to a pinch.

"Well, I must say!" she began, indignantly.

Then she broke off, looking hard at the female in the rose silk domino who stood at her elbow. In spite of the black lace mask which concealed the girl's face, Georgy was certain she knew her.

She began to say the girl's name, but another pinch, sharper than the first, arrested the word on her lips. Always quick-witted, Georgy realized that here must be some kind of emergency. She turned to her escort, and dismissed him with a plausible excuse. He went reluctantly, a little consoled by the fact that he was only leaving his charming partner in female company, at any rate.

"Now what is it?" hissed Georgy to her dark-haired companion. "And what on earth are you doing here anyway? I know you weren't invited, for you aren't acquainted with the Radleys."

"I — I must talk to you, Georgy." The other girl's lips were trembling so that she could scarcely form the words. "I need help, and there's no one to turn to — I went to your house, and the porter said you had come here to a — a masquerade. So I borrowed these things —" she indicated the mask and domino she was wearing — "and then I — I managed to slip in with some others, and — and hid outside the french windows, waiting for a chance to speak with you —"

"And that's where we had better go now," interrupted Georgy, decisively, "if we are not to be remarked. Take my arm, and try to look as if we'd just decided to step outside for a breath of air. I am dying to know what all this is about, my dear, but pray don't try to tell me until we are safe from eavesdroppers and prying eyes."

Mindful of what her brother had said earlier about the distinctive colour of her hair, Georgiana quickly drew her hood over her tell-tale auburn curls. It was simple enough for the two girls to slip out of the crowded room without being noticed. Once on the terrace, Georgy drew her friend down the steps, and along the path to a seat shaded from view by flowering trees.

"Now," she said, encouragingly, "what is all this about?" For answer, her companion burst into tears.

Georgiana's strong young arms drew the slighter figure close in a comforting grasp.

"There, there!" she soothed. "Very well, have a good cry, then. You shall tell me presently."

At these words, the other girl raised her tear-stained face. "No," she gulped, "there isn't much time — *he* may come out here again at any moment — or *they* may come after me — I left a note —"

She broke down again, shaking with heavy sobs that seemed to come from the very depths of her being.

"They?" repeated Georgy, puzzled. "Who do you mean? Who will come after you?"

"My — my — Mrs. Fyfield and her daughter," sobbed the girl. "I — I didn't tell them — where I meant to go — but — but — they might find out — somehow —"

"Don't put yourself in such a taking, my love," soothed Georgy. "Whatever has occurred? And who," she asked, as another thought struck her, "is this mysterious man who you seem to fear may come out here at any minute? Is it —" here Georgy gave free rein to her natural love of drama — "is it that your aunt is trying to force you into marriage with someone you detest? Is that it, Sue?"

"N-no," Susan gulped, trying desperately to gain control of herself. "It is worse than that —"

"Worse!" echoed Georgy, in awestruck tones, while her mind quickly ranged over every imaginable horror that could befall a gently-bred young girl.

"Yes, worse," repeated Susan, swallowing hard. "You see, it's all my own fault — at least, not *quite* all. But the worst part is due to — to — my own folly and impulsiveness. Oh, Georgy!" She broke into a heartrending wail, and buried her face on her friend's shoulder. "It's your brother Hugh — the Beau —

whom I fear may come out here again! He nearly caught me while — while I was waiting outside on the terrace!" She raised her head slightly, and finished, in a choking voice, "I — I love him, Georgy, and — and I never want to see him again! You must help me — please — help me to hide away from him! For I shall die — die of shame, I tell you — if — if he marries me, now!"

Chapter XI: Beau Eversley Amuses Himself

Beau Eversley slept late on the following morning and was awakened by his man bringing in the morning chocolate and some letters.

"This was delivered earlier by hand, sir," he said, indicating the top one, "but I did not care to disturb you."

Eversley idly turned the letter over in his hand, then, failing to recognize the handwriting, tossed it aside in favour of the rest of his correspondence. There being nothing of any particular interest, he eventually picked up the discarded letter, and broke the seal.

He looked for the address, but saw there was none. His curiosity piqued, he read the brief lines quickly, a frown gathering on his face as he did so.

I do not know how Best to say this, so Pray forgive me if I should unwittingly give Offence. There is no need of waiting Today on Mrs. Fyfield, for I shall not be present. I have decided to leave London for a Time, and I think it Best if you and I should never meet again.

It was most Kind in you, dear Sir — here there was a watery blot on the paper — *to agree to my foolish Deception, and I am deeply Grateful. But there is no longer any Purpose in continuing it, and I beg that you will speedily and for ever Forget one who has no name with which to sign this letter other than —*

S.

The words "for ever" had been underlined, and his eye persisted in dwelling on them even after he had read the letter twice, and had thoroughly mastered its contents.

He leapt out of bed, jerked his dressing gown about his shoulders, and strode over to the windows. For a time he stood gazing down abstractedly into the street, heedless of his man moving round the room laying out his garments.

So this was to be the end of the curious affair — an affair which had looked like ending in matrimony. No doubt about it, he reflected; if he had gone today to see Mrs. Fyfield's lawyer, it would have been to make a formal application for Susan's hand. He could see no other way. A much more brutal man than himself might have found it difficult to extricate himself from the net which chance had cast about him. It could not be done without causing further suffering to the girl; and she had suffered too much already.

He frowned suddenly. How great was the sacrifice he had been prepared to make for her sake? Would he have been ready to marry her whatever her parentage might be? He paused for a moment in his reflections, brought up short by the question. Something, after all, was owing to his family. An Eversley must marry his own kind.

No matter: the question need no longer vex him. Susan had gone away for a while, a wise course doubtless suggested by Mrs. Fyfield, who was not nearly such a henwitted female as she appeared to be. When the girl eventually returned, it was certain that she would view everything in a different light. At seventeen, he mused with a smile, even a few days could make a difference to one's outlook. A few weeks must succeed both in reconciling her to a new identity and in helping her to forget the schoolgirl fancy which had fixed itself on Beau Eversley. Who could tell? Perhaps while she was away she might even meet some eligible young man who could teach her the joy of sharing a more substantial love.

A brief picture of her flashed before his mind's eye — the piquant, childlike face framed in dark curls, the dreamy eyes, soft and deep. Suddenly he crushed the letter in his hand. She had been more fortunate than she knew in escaping marriage to her Beau ideal. Pedestals were notoriously precarious perches for such as he. There had been something about the child, some quality of freshness and naïveté, which had drawn out an answering protectiveness in him. She was the first female ever to inspire such feelings — except, of course, for his sisters. That was it, he told himself; he thought of Susan as a sister.

He thrust the crumpled note into the pocket of his dressing gown, and turned abruptly from the window. What should he do today? He felt the need of something to give his thoughts a new direction. What better than to resume the pursuit of Maria McCann?

He was not at all sure that she would be willing to receive him, but no trace of this appeared in his manner when he handed a card to the footman who answered her door.

He was invited to enter, and left cooling his heels for almost twenty minutes in a small, pleasant parlour on the ground floor. After consulting his watch for the third time, he was about to leave when he heard a quiet footstep outside the room. A moment later, Maria McCann entered.

She came towards him with a soft swish of skirts. Her gown was of pale pink muslin, with narrow stripes of grey, and she wore a pink ribbon threaded through her glossy black hair. Even in the unkind morning light which streamed through the windows, today she could have passed for six and twenty. It flashed across his mind that in reality she must be some ten years or so older — he would have taken his oath that her dark hair owed something to art. At once, he was annoyed with himself for allowing such thoughts to intrude at a moment when he was bent on once more insinuating himself into the lady's good graces.

"I was just about to leave," he said, carelessly, bowing over her hand. "I thought perhaps you were too occupied to see me today — or else that you did not wish to do so."

"Now why should you be after thinking that?" She put her head on one side, and surveyed him from under her long, black lashes.

"You know very well why," he replied, changing his tone. "Is it too soon to hope for your forgiveness? I came to see if I might by any means persuade you to drive with me for a while in the Park."

"Did you now? And what means had you in mind to make use of, I wonder?"

He hesitated for only a second, then drew her to him.

"Why, this means, my pretty."

His mouth came down on hers. She yielded for a brief moment, then pushed him playfully away.

"Ach, away with you, now!" The Irish lilt was very pronounced. "Sure, and it's myself should be sending you about your business, for divil a bit of good you are to any woman, and yourself such a shocking flirt. And what have you done, pray, with that little colleen who was with you yesterday morning, looking at you with her heart in her eyes, like the sweet innocent she was?"

"I did not come here to speak of her," he answered, with restraint in his manner.

"That I'll be bound! But some speaking there must be, whether you like it or not, for I'll not have you for escort if she is to be looking on and suffering agonies of jealousy, poor child!"

"My actions are really no concern of Miss — er — of the young lady in question." The height of his tone had increased noticeably. "But, if you must know, she is out of Town at present."

"And so you come to me?" Her lively eyes teased him.

"I see you choose to amuse yourself at my expense," he said, relaxing a little. "I suppose it is no more than I deserve for forgetting my appointment with you yesterday. As I told you then, this young lady means nothing to me."

She glanced at him shrewdly.

"Are you quite sure you do not protest too much?"

He frowned and looked away; for a second he made no answer.

Her mood changed suddenly. "Well, then, I'll surely forgive you, since it's a beautiful day, and I feel above all things in the mood for a drive in the Park. I'll away to fetch my bonnet, and then I'll be with you before you can turn around." At the door, she paused, "What horses are you driving — the greys or the chestnuts?"

"The greys."

"Then I'll take them in hand for a spell. You once promised me I might — remember?"

He bowed. "Can I ever forget anything you have said to me?"

"Ah, away with you!" she countered, with a sweep of her arm that eloquently expressed disbelief. "Sure, an' you've kissed the Blarney stone!"

When she returned, she had donned a pretty pick bonnet trimmed with grey feathers. She peeped at him so roguishly from under its brim, that his spirits, which had become unaccountably low once she had left him alone, lifted again.

The Park was crowded, not only with vehicles, but with people strolling. On such a lovely day, all fashionable London seemed to have turned out to take the air. Glances of curiosity and sometimes envy were thrown at the pair in the curricle.

"I see Beau Eversley's got the McCann in tow again," remarked a friend who was strolling with Peter Radley, as the equipage swept past them. "I thought he'd dropped her, and I hoped there might be a chance for someone else."

"There are quite a few in the running," replied Radley, with a shrug. "Whenever I happen to meet the lady, she seems to have a different escort. I collect she never goes out with the same man twice."

"With the exception of Eversley. What is there about him that draws on all the women — even an experienced Cyprian like the McCann must be?"

"God knows — you'd need a female to answer that question for you. But I fancy from the way she's shaping that the McCann means to go to the highest bidder; so Hugh's personal charm is nothing to the purpose."

She was driving the greys now, with light hands that yet could hold the high-bred animals in check.

"Excellent!" approved the Beau. "I see you've been well taught. Do you keep an equipage of your own in Ireland?"

She nodded, keeping her eyes on the track ahead. "I've a phaeton. And sometimes I join the Hunt. I've been riding ever since I can remember — I love it. But it was my husband who taught me to handle a pair."

"Your husband?"

She bit her lip, and for a moment her attention wandered. It was long enough for the spirited horses to feel the lack of guidance: they swerved suddenly.

"Careful!"

His hands came firmly down over hers, and he drew the horses to a standstill.

"Do you wish to continue?" he asked, quietly.

She shook her head. "No, I have lost patience, now. You drive."

They changed places, and for a time continued in silence.

"I did not know you were married," he said, at last, with some constraint in his manner.

"You did not need to know. I was but a short while a wife, and have been long a widow."

A look of relief crossed his face. It was not his way to dally with married women, even those of the McCann variety.

"Was your late husband also an actor?" he asked presently, in a casual tone. She did not answer for a moment; and, when she did, he saw that she disliked the question.

"No, he was not. But the past is done, and I'll not be talking of it now. I must be at the playhouse tonight, so you'd best take me home."

"May I see you again?"

"To be sure," she answered, carelessly.

"When? Tomorrow?"

She shook her head. "I am engaged for tomorrow."

"Then the next day?"

"Perhaps."

"What use is perhaps? Give me leave to meet you from the playhouse, and take you somewhere for supper."

"And where would you take me?"

"To my own house, for preference," he replied, quickly. "I have an excellent chef in my service — I'll wager you won't dine better anywhere."

She nodded. "And afterwards?"

He shot her a quick, sidelong glance from his keen hazel eyes.

"Who knows?" he said, softly.

"I do — I know." Her voice was emphatic. "Tell me, now, sir, how long have you played this game of love and leave?"

"For ever — till I met you," he replied, smiling.

"Away wi' ye! I am nothing — no more than the others — and you know it well, in your heart of hearts. One day you will meet someone who will truly matter to you."

"You may be right," he admitted, with a careless shrug. "But until that day comes? —"

He looked a question.

"You may be my escort — no more, mind. As for snug little suppers at your house —" She shook her head.

He stared at her for a moment, then threw back his head and laughed softly.

"Upon my word, you are the most extraordinary female!"

"Why?" She gave him a straight look. "Did you suppose that I was hanging out for a protector? Just because I am an actress, is that any reason to think me a — a lightskirt?"

"Phew!" he exclaimed, taken aback. "You don't mince your words, do you?"

"That I do not. But you must take me as you find me, or leave me alone."

"I'll take you," he said, with a smile.

"It will not be for long," she said. "My theatrical engagements here will be finished at the end of this month, and then I'll be away again to my own country."

"So soon? But you only arrived here quite recently — sturdy it was scarce worth your while to come to London for so short a spell?"

"I did not come only for my bookings at the playhouse. There was another reason."

He raised his brows, inviting an explanation.

"A private reason," she said, firmly. "But — it has come to nothing, and I may as well return."

"You don't wish to confide in me? Mayhap I could be of assistance — who knows?"

She shook her head, and deliberately changed the subject.

During the ensuing weeks, Beau Eversley saw a great deal of Maria McCann; but he quickly realized that there was no prospect of making her his mistress. It was a novel experience to one whom most women found irresistible. It might have been supposed that he would drop her, and try his luck in a more hopeful quarter. Oddly enough, he continued to seek her out, and for the moment showed no particular inclination for the company of any other female. The truth was that for the first time in his life he had found it possible to be on terms of platonic friendship with a woman, without any risk of emotional complications. The experience provided a relaxing interlude. Maria was a lively, intelligent companion who stimulated his mind; and as she always looked decorative, it exactly suited his cynical turn of humour to sport her on his arm under the envious glances of other men who fancied that he had succeeded where they had failed.

Besides, he needed something to divert his thoughts. At odd moments, they had an unsettling trick of turning to Susan. Where was she, and how was she faring? Possibly by now she had learnt her true identity, and become reconciled to it, whatever it might be. Poor child, she had paid a high price for her foolish hoax, and one which could not have been foreseen. Perhaps the experience would have made her less impetuous for the future. He wondered a trifle wistfully if this might not rob her of some of her charm; and then told himself impatiently that it was no concern of his.

He had been musing in this way one day when his man announced a visitor.

"A Mrs. Fyfield, sir. Shall I admit her?"

Beau Eversley tossed aside the newspaper he had been trying to read. His face betrayed his sudden interest.

"By all means," he said, starting to his feet. "Is Mrs. Fyfield alone?"

"Except for her maid, sir. Shall I show the lady in here?"

Hugh nodded, concealing an irrational feeling of disappointment. A moment later, Mrs. Fyfield entered the room. He asked her to be seated, and began the usual polite inquiries about her health, but she quickly broke into his civilities with a flustered note in her voice.

"Oh, you are very kind, Mr. Eversley! I do trust you will forgive my intruding on you in this way, but I do not quite know what should be done; and I thought perhaps you ought to be consulted, as, after all, you are an interested party."

Beau Eversley knitted his brows. "Forgive me, but I do not quite —"

"Oh dear! How foolish I am! I should have informed you at once that I am come about my — about Susan. Did she write you, sir? She told me that she meant to do so."

She looked anxiously at him, and he nodded. A gleam of hope came to her eyes.

"Oh, then, perhaps you know — can you tell me, Mr. Eversley, where Susan has gone?"

For a moment, he stared.

"Can I tell you — but do you mean to say, ma'am, that you yourself do not know?"

She shook her head despondently. "No. I have no notion where she has been since she left my house more than a fortnight ago."

Chapter XII: A Woman Called Polly

"No notion —" He broke off, knitting his brows. "But this is absurd! Do you mean to tell me that Miss F — that — er — Susan — ran away?"

Mrs. Fyfield nodded unhappily. "Exactly so! And I see that you do not know any more about where she has gone than I do myself. So there's no use in plaguing you with questions. Only I did hope, when she mentioned having written to you, that she might have divulged her plans to you. However, I see it isn't so, and now I just do not know what to do. For she's such a wild, impetuous girl, Mr. Eversley; and there's no saying what starts she may be getting up to, at this very minute, while we are sitting here talking!"

"I'm not so sure of that," he replied, soothingly. "I think it likely that certain of her recent experiences may have taught her the danger of acting on impulse. But suppose you tell me all about it from the beginning."

"Well, of course you'll recall that distressing scene when I had to confess that Susan was not my niece — after you'd left us, I persuaded her to go and lie down in her room. Sometimes a woman needs a shoulder to cry on, and other times she does better alone; and I judged this was one of the times when Susan needed to be alone for a while. Well, we went up to her at intervals, both my daughter and myself; but she'd locked her door, and only told us to go away and not bother her. When it was time for dinner, we both tried to tempt her downstairs without making the least headway, so in the end I had the housekeeper carry up a tray to her room. Susan took it in, but she doesn't seem to have eaten much from it — only a nibble here and there."

Beau Eversley nodded. "Understandably. And when did you find that she had gone, ma'am?"

"Oh, not until the next morning —"

"The next morning?" he repeated, amazed. "But by that time the child had been alone in her room for half a day and a whole night!"

"Yes, but you see, sir," replied Mrs. Fyfield defensively, "we both thought that she wanted to be left alone, and that in the end that would be the best thing for her. About seven o'clock, after the tray had been removed from outside her room, I went up once more and knocked. Again, she told me to go away — she said there was nothing she wanted, and she meant to get into bed presently. After that, Cynthia's betrothed — a Mr. Beresford — I think you are not acquainted with him — called on us. We all sat in the back parlour, which is cooler than the one that looks on the street — and I did not go near Susan's room again until Cynthia and I were about to retire for the night. Then I tapped gently on the door, but, receiving no answer, tried the handle. The door was still locked; so, thinking Susan must be in bed and asleep, I retired to my own room."

"Was the door of Susan's room still locked in the morning?" asked Eversley.

"Yes. When she didn't appear at breakfast, I asked the housemaid to knock on her door. The girl came down to say she could get no answer, so I went up myself. After knocking and shouting until I was quite exhausted, I became alarmed, and opened the door with the housekeeper's set of keys. There was no sign of Susan, and the bed was all made up as though no one had slept in it — and then I saw the letter, propped up on her dressing table. I can tell you it was a most unpleasant shock, Mr. Eversley!"

"I'm sure it was, ma'am. What did she say in this letter?"

"It was quite short — only a few lines. She said that she was going away for a short while, but would not tell me where, as she was particularly anxious that you shouldn't find out where she was. She said she meant to break off the engagement between you, and was writing to inform you of this. She finished by saying I was not to worry, for she would be somewhere *quite safe* — she underlined that three times. At the end of the letter —" the tears started to Mrs. Fyfield's eyes — "she wrote 'Thank you for all your kindness to me in the past. Your affectionate friend' — all my kindness, indeed! Why, I assure you, Mr. Eversley, I thought of that child as my own niece — I even do so now, and am consumed with anxiety on her behalf!"

"Quite needlessly, I am sure, ma'am," said the Beau, with more assurance than he felt. "Tell me, do you know if Susan took any money, or clothing?"

Mrs. Fyfield nodded. "Yes, we had lately been buying some new garments for her with money supplied by her lawyer. Most of these were missing, and her small portmanteau was gone, too. There had been a sum of money left over from our purchases, and this I had handed into her own keeping some days previously, so she most likely took that along with her. At any rate, I could find no trace of it — for I thought it best to search her room in order to reassure myself that she had not just run off with nothing but the clothes she stood up in!"

"I must confess that was in my own mind," admitted Eversley. "Have you consulted your lawyer at all?"

"Oh, yes! I went to Mr. Watson at once, for I felt that Susan was in trust to me, so to speak. Really, it must seem such a very odd situation to anyone else, but I have come to accept it over the years — is it not surprising, sir, how one can become accustomed to the most unusual circumstances? I often think —"

"Yes, indeed." He was quick to interrupt this philosophical flight, knowing how easy it was for his visitor to wander from the point. "But what did Mr. Watson have to say?"

"Why, he seemed to be not the least little bit put out. But then, you know, he is not a demonstrative man, and I cannot imagine he would ever get into a taking about anything under the sun!"

"How did you explain the matter to him, ma'am?"

"Well, of course, I could think of no better way to explain it than by telling him the truth — or most of it, at any rate," she added, hastily. "I said that a suitor had approached me for Susan's hand — but didn't give any name. I thought perhaps in the circumstances —" She hesitated, and gave him a long, considering look.

He raised his brows, inviting her to continue.

"Well, you know," she went on candidly, "I've had time to give everything a deal of thought since Susan disappeared; and I'm beginning to wonder if, after all, she might not have been telling the truth — the second time, I mean, when she insisted that she'd made it all up about your being betrothed. The only trouble is —"

She stopped again, searching his face with a surprisingly shrewd look in her eyes.

"Yes?" His expression was inscrutable.

She realized that he did not intend to help her.

"The trouble is, that I don't quite see why you should have confirmed her story, and actually come to me to ask for permission to address her, unless you really had been secretly engaged to her. I can't think of any other reason why you should go to such lengths — and yet I have a strong feeling that it was all a take-in! Forgive me if I am wrong, but —"

"Perhaps we could return for a moment to Mr. Watson — with your permission, ma'am. Having learnt of the circumstances and their outcome, what did he suggest you should do?"

"Well, first of all he was for doing nothing. I gave him Susan's letter to read, and he said it was obvious from it that she had some particular destination in mind — most likely the home of a relative or friend — and that she could come to no harm, and would no doubt return in a short time, feeling much better about the whole affair. But I think he must have seen that I still didn't feel easy in my mind; so then he said there could be no harm if I inquired discreetly among our relatives and friends to see if I could trace her."

"And this you have done?"

"Yes. It was a simple matter; for, as I think I explained to you before, I was always careful to keep Susan away from anyone who had known my family in the days before I took her into my care. As for friends — although she made several while she was at Miss Fanchington's seminary, she never visited at their homes. That left only those of my own friends whom she had met during the school holidays — and I cannot say that she ever reached that degree of intimacy with any of them which would lead her to plant herself on their doorsteps without so much as an invitation!"

"But you did make discreet inquiries, nevertheless?"

"Oh, yes. I declare, I have never paid so many calls for long enough! And it all had to be done so carefully, as you will appreciate — I had no wish to give anyone the slightest notion that Susan had run away. However, I think I may say —" she finished, not without a certain pride — "that no one suspected anything was amiss. And I am confident that she is not with any of them."

He frowned. "Nevertheless, her letter to you led the lawyer to believe that she had a definite destination in mind. The question is, where?" He paused for a moment, and a light came into his hazel eyes. "It might not be a bad notion to ask my sister what she knows of this." Another pause, then he shook his head. "But no! There isn't the slightest possibility that Susan could have seen Georgy — that is, if you are certain that she didn't leave the house during that afternoon."

"Oh, no! As I told you, Mr. Eversley, Cynthia and I were constantly going up to her room, and talking to her."

"Except for the period after seven o'clock, when Mr. Beresford called on you, and you assumed that Susan had retired for the night," he said, thoughtfully. "Now, let me see... No, I am confident that it would have been impossible. I myself escorted my sister to a masquerade that evening."

"Indeed, sir, I never seriously considered it! For, as she says she wishes above all things to keep out of your way, it would scarcely serve her turn to go and stay with your sister."

"Perhaps not — although I must confess I am not such a frequent caller at my parents' home as you might suppose, ma'am. However, you may be right. I should be bound to hear of it, if she were there. Well, it seems for the moment that we are unable to solve the mystery."

Mrs. Fyfield sighed. "I came to you as a last resort, hoping that perhaps she might have changed her mind, and told you where she was going. What do you think I should do now, Mr. Eversley? For she's been gone over a fortnight, and I am bound to be anxious, no matter how calm Mr. Watson may be about the business!"

"He is probably right," replied the Beau, drawing a handsome blue and gold snuff box from his pocket and regarding it abstractedly for a few moments. "Tell me, ma'am, did he make any disclosures to you about the young lady's parentage?"

"Nothing to the purpose. It seems that throughout he has been acting upon instructions received from a client at the time when Susan first came to me. He pointed out that he was not at liberty to reveal the name of this client, nor the nature of what had passed between them —"

"Very proper, of course," nodded Hugh, taking snuff in a deliberate manner, and returning the box to his pocket. "There is nothing, however, to prevent him from seeking his client's permission to acquaint you with these particulars."

"So he said on my first visit, and he undertook to do that very thing. But when I waited on him again yesterday, he told me that it was of no use. His client positively refused to divulge anything."

Beau Eversley was thoughtful, tapping his fingers; on the arm of his chair.

"I wonder, ma'am, did you by any chance point out to Mr. Watson that this attitude of his client's might make it difficult to — er — arrange a suitable marriage for Susan?"

"Indeed I did. For, of course, I do realize, always supposing —" she darted a shrewd look at him — "that an engagement really does exist between you, that a gentleman in your position would scarce feel disposed to wed a nameless girl. If it should chance to turn out that she is the natural daughter of a gentleman of birth, there would not be much harm done, even if it isn't quite what one would like. After all, Horry Walpole's niece, the Countess of Waldegrave, was Sir Edward Walpole's natural daughter, and no one ever thought any the worse of her for that. Indeed, Joshua Reynolds painted her three daughters, as you doubtless know, and the picture was exhibited at the Royal Academy — so what could be more respectable than that, I ask you?"

"I must confess I cannot at present think of anything," replied the Beau, dryly.

"Yes, but suppose Susan should turn out to be the daughter of a mere nobody — or — or worse? What then?" pursued Mrs. Fyfield.

"What indeed?"

"However, Mr. Watson naturally does not know who Susan's suitor is, and so he doesn't quite view the matter in that light," continued Mrs. Fyfield. "He can see no reason why I shouldn't do what his client recommends, and continue to represent Susan as my niece, just as I have done all these years."

"You did not then tell him that you had revealed the truth to me, as well as to Susan?"

Mrs. Fyfield looked a little sheepish. "Well, no, I did not," she confessed. "I was anxious at all cost to keep your identity secret —"

Hugh Eversley nodded. "I appreciate your discretion, ma'am. But does not Mr. Watson's mysterious client desire to know something about the man who is seeking to marry his protégée?"

She shook her head in bewilderment. "That's the oddest part of it — it seems that this man (for I suppose it must be a man?) doesn't want to trouble his head with the affair at all. Mr. Watson told me that his client's latest instructions were that he might marry the girl to anyone whom he saw fit — providing it was not to a known fortune-hunter."

"So Mr. Watson has not even taken you into his confidence as regards the sex of his client?"

"No. But surely it must be a man? I cannot believe, though," said Mrs. Fyfield, thoughtfully, "that he would be Susan's father, natural or otherwise. Surely no parent could be quite so indifferent to the fate of his offspring?"

The Beau shrugged. "As to that, ma'am, there are some very odd people in the world."

"I am beginning to believe it. But what should I do now, Mr. Eversley? I cannot endure any longer not to know where Susan is! I declare, I find myself quite unable to take the interest I should in my own daughter's approaching marriage — I cannot dismiss Susan from my mind!"

Beau Eversley reflected that Mrs. Fyfield was not the only one in this situation. It suddenly came home to him how many times his own thoughts had turned to Susan over the past weeks. He stood up abruptly.

"Then I think we must find her, Mrs. Fyfield. After we've done so, I am sure you'll agree it will be for her to decide if she wishes to return to you at once, or after an interval."

"Oh, yes!" replied Mrs. Fyfield, eagerly. "As long as she is staying somewhere suitable, I shall not mind at all! It is only the anxiety of not knowing where she is that quite cuts up my peace of mind!"

"Exactly so." He paused, a frown of concentration on his brow. "I think, you know, ma'am, that it will not do for her to remain in ignorance of her parentage. Evidently it is useless to expect any help from the lawyer on that head. Are you quite sure that you can throw no light on the mystery yourself? There might be some small detail which you can recollect — did the child bring any personal possessions with her when she came to you, for instance?"

Mrs. Fyfield shook her head. "Nothing I can think of — excepting, of course, the clothing she was wearing. And that has been thrown out these many years!"

"No toys? Nor trinkets?" Again she shook her head. He sighed. "A pity. There might have yielded some clue to her identity." He broke off, as another thought crossed his mind. "How did the child come to you? Who brought her?"

"Why, Mr. Watson, to be sure! I well remember it was a bitterly cold day, and poor little Susan was crying, what with cold and fatigue — and the abigail who was holding the child did not look in much better case herself. They brought her in a closed carriage, after dark. Cynthia had been some time abed — she was only six years old, then, you know, Mr. Eversley — and I remember her nurse grumbling that Susan's crying would waken her. However, it didn't, and Nurse soon had little Susan quiet and safely tucked up. Although I recollect that Nurse did tell me that the child used to wake and cry in the night for long enough after that — it seems she was asking for someone called Polly. I had to tell Nurse that this was the name of Susan's own nurse at her old home; for, of course, Nurse thought Susan was my brother's child, and that I knew all about her past life."

"Naturally. And I dare say your surmise was correct." He began to pace slowly up and down the room.

"Polly," he repeated, thoughtfully. "The name of a nursemaid. Not much to go on. Polly — from — where?" Suddenly he turned to his visitor, speaking in a brisker tone. "Did they chance to let slip the name of the place from which they'd collected the child?"

Mrs. Fyfield hesitated. "Not as far as my recollection goes — though it's so very long ago, I might well have forgotten. But you may be sure that Mr. Watson would not let slip anything he didn't wish me to know. I tell you what, though, Mr. Eversley," she added, with a flash of inspiration, "the abigail who was with him might have made some such communication to Nurse; for she went off with Nurse after Susan was settled in bed, and they took some refreshment together, while Mr. Watson and I were discussing the arrangements about the child."

"Do you know where this woman can be found?"

"Nurse? Oh, yes. She lives in the village of Islington — I go to visit her sometimes, for she was with me from the time of Cynthia's birth until Susan went to school, and one cannot quite cast off an old servant, you know."

"Do you think, ma'am, it might be possible to ask her about this matter without betraying the reason for your interest in it?"

"Oh, yes, I am certain of it!" exclaimed Mrs. Fyfield, with a touch of pride. "Do you know, Mr. Eversley, I find I have quite a talent for dissimulation — is it not shocking?"

Chapter XIII: More Than a Sister

Lady Eversley was not at home when her eldest son called on her later that morning.

"It doesn't signify," he told the butler. "Is my sister here?"

"Miss Georgiana is at present staying in the country with Mrs. Cunningham, sir."

Beau Eversley stared. "The devil she is! When did she leave Town?"

"More than a fortnight since, Mr. Eversley. She journeyed to Richmond with Mrs. Cunningham." The man waited a moment, while Hugh stood there frowning, then added, "Can I convey any message from you to her ladyship when she returns?"

Hugh started. "No, it's of no consequence. I'll look in again."

He left the house and slowly descended the steps to the street. Georgy in Richmond — it was incredible! What on earth could have possessed her? He well remembered how she had poured scorn on Evelina for leaving the diversions of the Town. She must have had some powerful incentive to take such a course herself. It might be worth while to look into her motives.

Once he had reached this conclusion, he lost no time in setting out for Richmond, and arrived at his sister's house in the early afternoon.

It seemed to take some time to find the mistress of the house, but she came to him at last, and welcomed him affectionately.

"Hugh! I declare it's an age since you were last here! There's nothing amiss, I trust — Mama is well?"

"My dear Evelina, you know perfectly well that our mother is blessed with an excellent constitution. How are the children?"

"Oh, they go on famously! You will not know Tony, he is grown so tall — and even little Jane —"

"I must see them, my dear. By the way, I understand that Georgy is staying here?"

Evelina's face clouded. "Ye-es," she admitted.

"What persuasion did you use to bring her?" he asked, smiling. "Only a few days before you left Town, she was saying that nothing would induce her to shut herself away in the country, as you were about to do."

Evelina shrugged uneasily. "Stuff! There is always plenty going on in Richmond; as you know. We are not without neighbours, after all. But you know Georgy — she is a creature of impulse."

"Perhaps. But there's usually method in her madness. Where is she, by the way? I wonder she has not come to meet me."

"Oh — she is in the garden with — with George," said Evelina, hesitantly.

"George!" He stared. "What the devil is he doing here? The term is not yet ended."

"Well — I fancy there was some trouble, and he has been sent down until next term — but not a word to Papa, mind, Hugh! I promised to keep him here until the term ends, when he may safely put in an appearance at home. It's not much longer now, and there's no point in putting Papa into a passion."

"Silly young fool," said Hugh, casually. "Was that why Georgiana came here, then?"

She hesitated for a moment. "No, for George did not arrive until a day or two after we did," she admitted at last.

"Quite a family gathering," he said, dryly. "Shall we step outside and join them?"

"Oh, but surely you will want something to drink after driving all that way in this heat!" exclaimed Evelina, in a distracted way. "Only tell me what you will take, and after I've ordered it for you I'll go and fetch the others."

"Thank you, my dear; you may procure me a tankard of ale, and I'll take it in the garden with the rest of the family. It will be cooler out of doors."

As he spoke, he turned towards the french windows which opened on to the garden.

"Oh, but," stammered his sister, holding on to his arm, "I think perhaps I should go first and let them know that you are here."

He looked at her in amazement "Why on earth should you do so? Do you imagine they will wish to change their dress in my honour? A fine thing, if I must be announced to my own brother and sister!"

"Well, I —"

"Say no more, Eve." He shook her off gently, and, walking over to the windows, pushed them open and stepped outside. "Do you know, I find myself suddenly impatient to set eyes on them?"

"But —"

She darted after him, pulling ineffectually at his arm. He stopped, and disentangled himself from her clutches.

"If I might persuade you *not* to maul my coat —" he protested, gently. "Surely Cunningham has taught you better in all this time?"

"I'm sorry —"

She broke away from him suddenly, and went darting down the steps in the direction of a small formal garden enclosed by clipped hedges.

"Georgy!" She raised her voice. "George! Here is Hugh come to see us!"

Beau Eversley could not help smiling at his sister's antics. They served to confirm the suspicion which had brought him post-haste to Richmond. He made no comment, however, but followed closely on her heels as she approached a small arbour, the interior of which was almost concealed from view by a profusion of yellow climbing roses. His smile broadened as he watched his younger brother and sister hastily leave the shelter of the arbour in response to Eve's summons, and come quickly across the lawn towards him.

"What a pleasant family party we are, to be sure," he drawled. "George, I collect, has been sadly misunderstood at college and has sought refuge with his elder sister."

"Don't trouble to exercise your wit on me, Hugh — you might get the worse of the encounter," warned George, with a grin that was a little sheepish.

"Do you think so?" Hugh countered, in a tone of incredulity. "Ah, well, never mind. *Your* presence here is accounted for, but I must confess myself puzzled at Georgy's."

"I — I — wanted a change of air," Georgiana said hurriedly, kissing him. "But, as for that, why are you here, Hugh?"

"You are right, of course," he parried. "Attack *is* the best method of defence."

She gave a forced laugh. "So now I am to defend myself for visiting my own sister! What next will you think of, Hugh, I wonder?"

"You need not wonder for long," he answered, abandoning his careless manner. "I've come to ask you a straight question,

Georgy, and I'd like a straight answer." He paused, watching her face. "Where is your friend Susan — er — Fyfield?"

She stared at him as though he had taken leave of his senses. It was very well done, he thought; but then Georgy had always been something of an actress.

"Susan? At home with her aunt, I imagine. How should I know? I've been out of Town for long enough."

He nodded as though satisfied; then turned suddenly on Evelina.

"And you, Eve? Have you seen the girl?"

She started, and glanced surreptitiously at the rose arbour.

"I? Oh — er — no — goodness — why should I?"

His eyes had followed the direction of her glance. Suddenly he strode across the lawn towards the arbour.

"I say, Hugh," said George, grabbing his arm. "I wish you would come and look at a mare I've just bought from a friend of mine. A rare bargain, I promise you — come and look her over, and see if you don't agree."

"No need," replied Hugh, shaking him off firmly. "I'll lay any odds you were taken in."

"No such thing," retorted George, indignantly, placing himself between his brother and the rose arbour. "Just slip round to the stables with me, and see if you don't eat your words!"

"I've no intention of going anywhere at present," said Hugh, flatly. "I mean to drink a tankard of ale in yonder shady arbour."

He took a step towards it, but George barred his way. "I shouldn't," he said, hurriedly. "No air in there — much cooler under the trees — let's go and sit —"

Hugh thrust George aside in the middle of his protests, and strode purposefully into the arbour before either of his sisters could prevent him.

He heard a stifled gasp as he entered, and caught sight of a figure in white muslin crouching behind the rustic seat which the arbour contained.

"So you are here," he said. "I thought as much. You may as well come out now — I am not quite as addicted to the game of hide and seek as you seem to be."

She moved from behind the seat and went out into the open, showing a flushed face to the others. George moved protectively to her side.

"Look here, Hugh, she don't wish to see you." He faced his brother defiantly. "I don't know why — I've no notion what tricks you've been up to — but she ain't obliged to see you if she don't want to, and that's that!"

"Dear me," said the Beau, gently. "You appear to have found yourself a champion, Miss Susan."

Susan put up an unsteady hand to brush a strand of dark hair from her eyes.

"George has been very kind to me," she answered, quietly. "So have Evelina and Georgy."

The Beau raised a quizzical eyebrow. "George?" he queried. "So you're on Christian name terms?"

"What do you expect?" laughed Georgiana. "They've been under the same roof for the past fortnight, taking their meals together, riding together — even playing cards together! I promise you, Sue is become quite one of the family."

"I see." His tone lacked expression.

"The thing is," said George, firmly, "Susan particularly desires to be left alone, so if you've come to badger her into returning to London, Hugh, you'll have me to reckon with."

"You terrify me," drawled the Beau.

His eyes rested thoughtfully on his younger brother's face. Although well into his twentieth year, so far George had never betrayed the slightest interest in any female. Like all the male Eversleys, he was a keen sportsman and spent the greater part of his vacations out of doors with friends of similar tastes. His behaviour towards Susan at Georgiana's coming-out party had been much more in character than this sudden access of interest in the girl's concerns. Hugh reflected wryly that it looked as though George had taken a tumble at last; he wondered how Susan might feel, and his glance moved to her.

She was standing close to George, so that their arms almost touched. It struck Hugh at once that she looked older in some indefinable way. Her face was a little thinner, and some of the piquancy had gone out of it. As Hugh watched her, she turned her face up to George with an expression of trust and affection in her eyes.

An unpleasant feeling suddenly seized the Beau in the pit of the stomach. He took a step towards them.

"Don't think I don't mean it, Hugh," warned George, on his mettle.

"My dear chap, of course you do," replied his brother, in a quiet tone. "Make yourself easy. I came only because Mrs. Fyfield desired me to ascertain, if I could, where her niece had gone; and I deduced from Georgy's absence that I might find Miss Susan here."

"That's Susan's aunt, ain't it?" asked George, puzzled. "Why the devil should she ask you to look for Susan, I'd like to know?" He turned to his sisters. "There's something dashed havey cavey going on here, and I'm not sure that you two don't know what it is! I don't mind telling you that for days past I've had more than a suspicion that there was something in the wind!"

"Dear George," said Georgiana, sweetly, "you are always so quick in the uptake!"

"No sauce from you, vixen!" He turned to Susan, and his tone softened. "Won't you tell me what all this is about? Believe me, I am yours to command in anything — and if you don't want Hugh here you have only to say!"

She shook her head. "Forgive me, George," she said, with a quiet dignity that the Beau had never noticed in her before, "but all I can tell you at present is that I — I became involved in a silly scrape through my own folly. Far from annoying me, your brother has tried to help me out of it."

"I wish you had come to me!" exclaimed George.

"I did not know you then as I do now," she replied, and Hugh winced inwardly. "But if you have no objection, all of you, I would like just to say a few words in private to Mr. Eversley."

"As long as you're quite sure —" began George, doubtfully.

She flashed a warm smile at him as she nodded. Reluctantly, he turned away with his sisters towards the house.

"Shall I send the ale out to you now?" asked Evelina, as they went.

"Later," replied Hugh.

For a moment, he watched their retreating figures. Then he turned to Susan.

"Shall we sit down?"

They entered the arbour, and sat side by side on the bench, amid the perfume of roses.

"I suppose you must have thought it very foolish in me to hide away from you," said Susan. "But I thought you had come on a chance visit, and if possible I wanted to keep my presence here a secret."

"On the contrary, I apologize for being obliged to inflict myself on you," replied the Beau, dryly. "But Mrs. Fyfield was becoming anxious at not hearing any news of you since you left a fortnight ago. She came to me thinking that I might know where you could be found."

"But," objected Susan, "she knew very well that I had not told you where I was going. I made a particular point of that in the letter I left for her."

"I think she felt you might have relented, you know," he said, smiling. "In any event, she was in a mood to clutch at straws."

"Poor Aunt Hattie!" exclaimed Susan, with a sigh. "I fear I have used her very ill! But it was such a dreadful shock — and I had to get away, so that I might think what was to be done."

"And have you now decided?" he asked, gently.

She nodded. "Yes. I think I must try to discover who I really am. I've been talking things over with Georgy and Evelina; and they feel, too, that this would be best, if it can be done. But it may not be possible," she added, in a less sanguine tone, "for I've written to Mr. Watson, and he can tell me nothing at all."

"Then that would explain why your — why Mrs. Fyfield did not find him alarmed at your absence. She went to see him when first you were missing, and later she complained to me that he had taken the whole matter very calmly — which, of course, was natural, when he knew all the time where you might be found."

"I did ask him to keep my direction from her for the time being," explained Susan. "Perhaps it was selfish of me, but —" She paused and coloured a little — "I felt I must go right away from — from everyone."

"And perhaps particularly from me?"

"Yes," she answered, looking down at her hands, which were clasped together in her lap. "I felt so — so ashamed!" she said, in a rush. "I had put you in such a — a false position, by my stupid folly, and then what Aunt Hattie revealed about my parentage only made matters worse! But not for anything could I have stayed there, and — and become an object of — of your — chivalry! The only thing to do was to go right away where you couldn't find me!"

It was on the tip of his tongue to tell her just how often his thoughts had turned to her during her absence; but he thought of the new understanding which he had noticed between George and herself, and he kept silent.

"So you came here," he said, after a pause. "How did you contrive it? It was the only thing that puzzled me when it first occurred to me that you might be in Richmond with my sisters. I could think of no way in which you could have seen my sister Georgy that day in order to enlist her aid."

"I saw her at the masquerade," said Susan, simply.

He was betrayed into surprise. "But how? And how could you know she would be there?"

She explained what had happened. He listened in silence; at the end an exclamation escaped him.

"You say you were loitering in the garden? But — in that case —"

He broke off, remembering the mysterious lady in the black lace mask whom he had pursued and kissed that same evening.

He stole a quick look at her, and saw that she was blushing.

"Never mind that," she said, uncertainly. "I contrived to slip into the ballroom, and find Georgy. I was wearing a mask and domino, and no one noticed me in all that crowd. And when I'd told Georgy what had happened, she recollected that her elder sister was to come to Richmond on the following day. So she slipped away from the masquerade for long enough to escort me to Evelina's Town house, and then went back to the Radleys' in time for you to take her in to supper. She said you would never notice her absence, and it seems you didn't."

"I shall certainly watch that young woman more closely if ever I'm such a gull as to escort her anywhere again," said Hugh, grimly. "It would have been all the same, I dare say, if she'd been planning an elopement! But to return — I collect you were then obliged to confide to a certain extent in my sister Evelina?"

"Yes. She has been so good — indeed, they all have!"

"It is not difficult to be good to you, Susan."

For a moment their eyes met. She turned quickly away. He felt a sudden impulse to take her in his arms, and restrained himself with difficulty.

"I collect that both my sisters are in your confidence, but you have not confided to any extent in my brother George?" he asked, with an effort to steer away from dangerous ground.

She shook her head. "I didn't want everyone to know. Besides, George —" She hesitated.

"Yes?" he asked, sharply.

"Oh, nothing. Only we have become such close friends — and he might despise me, if he knew."

He was about to remark cynically that George could ill afford to sit in judgement on anyone else for getting into a scrape; but again he refrained. If Susan had indeed outgrown her hero-worship of himself, and was beginning to entertain a more mature feeling for his younger brother, he must not throw any rub in the way. After all, had he not always believed and hoped that this very thing would happen eventually?

"I doubt if he would," Hugh contented himself with saying. "But perhaps it may be best not to take him into your confidence until you've solved this mystery about your parentage. How do you mean to set about it, since you've discovered that your lawyer cannot help you?"

She frowned. "Truth to tell, I don't know where to begin. I suppose if Aunt Hattie — I can't become accustomed to calling her by any other name! — if she had been able to tell me anything at all to the purpose, she would have done so on that dreadful day. So obviously there is no use in plaguing *her* with questions; and for the life of me, I can't think of anyone else who could help!"

"You might try me," he said, quietly.

She glanced quickly at him, and coloured. "You have been put to trouble enough on my behalf!" she replied, passionately. "When I think of the situation into which I forced you — I have thought of it often, since, and the mere recollection makes me squirm in shame! — I wonder that you can bear the sight of me!"

To his surprise, he found himself unable to answer her for a moment. He took a firm grip on himself.

"You take it all too seriously," he said, with forced lightness.

She looked abashed; too late he realized that his words had made her feel small, instead of conveying reassurance. He hastened to turn the conversation back into the original channel.

"What I really meant was that I am ready — no, eager — to help you, if you will only accept my assistance. I have already plagued your — er — Mrs. Fyfield — with questions, as you put it. She, too, I may say, is anxious to solve the riddle, for she holds you in as much affection as if you were truly her niece — of that you may be assured, Susan." He spoke the last words with emphasis, and had the satisfaction of seeing the hurt expression leave her eyes.

"I asked her if you had brought any possessions with you when you came," he continued. "I thought there might be some clue to your identity among them. However, it seems there was nothing. That was very remiss of you, don't you agree? The heroines in novels always contrive to have a locket or a ring, or something of the kind which will help to identify them."

He was rewarded by a faint laugh.

"But my questions did prompt Mrs. Fyfield to remember that when you first came to her you used to cry for someone called Polly — do you recollect the name, by any chance?"

She considered for a moment, then shook her head. "No, I cannot say I do."

"Well, most likely it wouldn't have taken us much further if you had, for we still would have to discover where this Polly lives — if, indeed, she is still alive and has not moved away since you were brought from her care. However, Mrs. Fyfield, who is, by the way, a most ingenious female! — has thought of something which may help." He went on to explain how Mrs. Fyfield thought her former nursemaid might possibly have some information.

"Of course," he concluded, "it's only a straw in the wind, but it might turn out to be helpful."

"And if it doesn't?" asked Susan.

"Then we'll think of something else," he said, energetically. "We'll find the answer, never fear."

"There is someone who knows the answer all the time," said Susan, slowly. "And that is the person who is Mr. Watson's client. Whoever that person is —" she went on, with a trembling lip, "whether my father or — or some other relative, one thing is clear. He — or she — doesn't wish to have anything to do with me at all."

She turned towards him, her dark eyes bright with threatening tears. In that moment, he knew at last that he no longer regarded Susan as a sister — if, in fact, he had ever done so. He longed to draw her into his arms and murmur words of comfort against her soft, dark hair. But he thought of his brother George, and of the understanding which appeared to be growing between these two. Instead, he patted her hand in elder brother style.

"You can't know that," he replied, consolingly. "There might be circumstances which would make it impossible for you to be received."

"I can think of one circumstance," she said, uncertainly. "And — and that — would make it impossible for anyone — ever to — to consider — me — as — as —"

In another moment, Beau Eversley's quite commendable control would have given way. But a shadow fell across the arbour, and George was standing there, holding a tray on which stood two silver tankards.

"We thought you'd had long enough," he began, "and Eve took pity on your thirst, Hugh — why, Susan!"

He broke off abruptly, setting the tray down clumsily on a small wooden table within the rose arbour. He turned on his brother angrily.

"You oaf, Hugh! What have you said to upset her so? Damned if I don't —"

"Watch your tongue!" returned Hugh, sharply, forgetting for a moment the need to treat George as an equal in front of Susan, and not as a younger brother. He recollected in time, and rising to his feet, lifted one of the tankards from the tray and carried it outside, leaving the two of them together in the arbour.

"What has he been saying to you, Sue?" asked George, bending over her in a protective way.

"Nothing," replied Susan. The interruption had staved off the threatening tears, leaving her a trifle irritable. "I wish you will not fuss so, George! It was not anything your brother said — it is just that I felt a trifle low — but I am all right now, I assure you!"

"Well, if you're certain," conceded George, reluctantly. "Only I'll not have him coming here," he added, raising his voice, "setting you at sixes and sevens! D'ye hear that, Hugh?"

The Beau raised his face from the tankard, and laughed gently. "Oh, yes. My hearing's always been excellent." He took another draught of ale. "This stuff's deuced good, old chap," he said. "Let me recommend you to come and take a damper."

George glowered for a moment, then glanced at Susan. She smiled back at him, and at once his expression lightened. He picked up his tankard; and raising it to her, drank deep.

Chapter XIV: Farewell

It was plain that Susan did not yet feel quite ready to return to her home in London; and when Evelina hospitably insisted that she should prolong her stay in Richmond she gave way thankfully, after an initial polite show of diffidence. Hugh, however, resisted all his sister's attempts to persuade him to remain with them for a few days. He pointed out that Mrs. Fyfield would be anxiously awaiting news of Susan, and also that he had had a number of engagements in Town. The truth was that he had no wish to stay and watch the daily strengthening of the attachment between Susan and George; but perhaps he did not admit this even to himself.

He returned to Town without delaying longer than was necessary for Susan to write a letter to Mrs. Fyfield. He was in a somewhat reckless mood, a rare thing for the nonchalant Beau Eversley, and drove as though pursued by the devil himself. Passing a south-bound Mail coach just outside Kew, he swept past it with barely an inch to spare, causing the stolid Mail coachman to describe his parentage in unflattering terms.

Arrived in Town, he went straight to Duke Street with Susan's letter. Mrs. Fyfield's relief at having news of her missing charge was sincere and uninhibited.

"As long as she is in safe hands, sir, she may stay away as long as she wishes — poor child, I've been thinking so much about her odd situation over these last few weeks, and one cannot but sympathize with her wish to go right away from everybody she knows! And for her to be with your sister, Mrs. Cunningham — why, of course, Mr. Eversley, nothing could be more suitable! Though even now I am not sure how much truth there is in that Banbury story she told me of your engagement — but, there, I'll not tease you with questions at present. You must be quite fatigued, and longing for your dinner after so much travelling — if you would do us the honour to sit down at our table, I can assure you we should both be delighted!"

The Beau politely but firmly refused. Mrs. Fyfield then told him of her intention to visit Nurse on the following day, and he asked if he might look in to hear the result of the interview. They agreed on a time, and he took his leave.

Several hours later, having changed his dress and dined, he called at the playhouse for Maria McCann. The reckless mood was still upon him, increased by the unusual quantity of wine he had taken with his solitary dinner. The lady cast a sharp glance at him as they settled down together in his town coach, and gave a low gurgle of laughter.

"Sure, an' I'll swear ye're just a bit on the go!" she teased.

"You don't mean to insinuate that an Eversley is incapable of carrying his liquor?" he asked, raising one eyebrow in his own particular mannerism.

"Be easy." She tapped his knee with the ivory fan she was carrying. "One would need to know you very well to discern it. But I have not seen you so, before. Have you just left a particularly gay party? Or is something amiss?"

"I dined alone," he answered, fingering a curl that danced on her cheek to the movement of the carriage.

"Then there is something wrong. Tell me."

"The only thing wrong," he replied, putting an arm about her and drawing her close to his side, "is the distance that you insist on maintaining between us."

She used the fan again, this time a little more sharply. "Sure, an' I thought we'd been over all that and had done with it! A fine thing, to start it all up again just as we'd reached a comfortable understanding — and myself away back to Ireland before long."

His arm tightened round her, and he laid his cheek against hers.

"Maria," he murmured, while his lips sought hers, "surely you cannot be so cold?"

A street lamp's glow slanted briefly across the interior of the coach, and caught the rich colour of his tawny hair.

Suddenly, she turned towards him in swift abandon, pressing her mouth to his. For a long moment they clung together, almost as if the embrace were a prelude to farewell.

Then he raised his head, and softly spoke her name. Gently, she disentangled herself from his arms.

"It will not do," she stated, simply.

He tried to take her in his arms again; but this time there was no yielding on her part.

"Why won't it do?" His tone held a hint of chagrin. "You have no need of returning to Ireland, and nothing else stands between us."

"I do have need of returning to my own country, for that is where my work lies. But, apart from that, there are two things that stand between us — or, I should say, two people."

"What people?" he asked, a trifle out of humour. "For my part, I know of no one."

"No?" She looked him straight in the eyes. "An actress perforce learns a deal about the emotions. When you kissed me just now, it was a kiss of desperation, as though in my arms you sought to forget some other woman."

"Fustian!" he drawled, recovering his poise. "You read too much into too little, my dear. I suppose you have the habit of dramatizing everything — an occupational hazard, perhaps."

"Perhaps. But in this instance, I'm prepared to wager —"

"Be careful," he warned her. "It will not be money I shall ask for, should you be the loser."

She took no notice of the interruption. "I would stake my last coin that you are in love with someone else. And I fancy," she added, thoughtfully, "that I know who it is."

"Then be so good as to inform me, for I have no idea!"

"Come, who is play-acting, now? You may as well admit that you are in love with that little schoolroom miss — what is her name? Susan — yes, that's it — Susan Fyfield."

"I've told you before that the child means nothing to me."

"Oh, yes, I know; and it was partly true, then, at least. But if I am not mistaken —"

"Which, of course, you *are* —"

"— you are now head over ears in love with her —"

"Stuff!" he retorted, forcibly. "If you must know, I have every expectation of seeing her eventually wed to a younger brother of mine."

She gave him a long, considering look. "So that is it," she said, in a satisfied tone. "Now that you've at last discovered you want her, you believe you've lost her to someone else. But you're faint and far off, dear Hugh. I could not at first be certain of your feelings in the matter, but I never had any doubt from the beginning that the child was completely infatuated by you."

He gave a short, bitter laugh. "Infatuation! Yes, that was it, right enough. You yourself may know how easily such a fantasy comes and goes."

She shook her head. "That I do not," she replied, with a wistful smile. "For when I was in the grip of such a feeling, I married the man who inspired it." She paused. "I have had causes enough since then to regret that marriage — and yet, in spite of all —"

"Is that your second person? Your dead husband? Is it he who stands between us, as you imagine Susan does?"

"No. For I am not so foolish as to look for such a love twice in a lifetime. One must be content with less," she said, softly. "Yet the other person I mention is the man I intend to marry."

"To marry!"

"Does that surprise you? Perhaps you think me fit only for a less binding connection?"

"No, not that — but —" He broke off, uncertain how to continue.

"Well, never mind what you think. The fact is that I am to wed the manager of a playhouse over the water — his name need not concern you. It will be a comfortable arrangement, for I shall still have my work, and we will each of us gain a companion who shares an abiding interest."

"Then why did you come to London at all?" he asked, puzzled. "If your future was already planned —"

"There was something I had to do, first," she interrupted him. "Something I had to know."

"You've mentioned this before," he said, with a quick frown. "I recollect you told me then that you had not succeeded in your mission — whatever that was."

She shook her head sadly. "No. I have still not succeeded. And now the time has come for me to leave."

"Won't you tell me what it is?" he urged. "I would like to assist you —"

She laid a cool hand over his. "Better not," she answered, slowly. "There's no saying what harm might be done —"

"Confound these mysteries!" he answered, impatiently. "Can't you trust me?"

"Implicitly, my dear. But there are others concerned." The coach slowed to a stop, and she pulled her gauze scarf about her bare shoulders. "And here is my lodging," she finished. "I must leave you."

"But wait! May I not accompany you indoors, at least?"

"Not in your present mood, my friend." Before he realized what she was about to do, she suddenly leaned over and planted the lightest of kisses on his cheek. Then she stood up as the coachman came to open the door.

"Sure, and we've had many good times together," she said, softly. "But perhaps this had better be our farewell."

Chapter XV: Family Likeness

Two days later, Beau Eversley was back in Richmond with news which he hoped might carry Susan a stage further towards solving the riddle of her parentage.

He found her playing hide and seek in the garden with Evelina's small children, and experienced some difficulty in persuading them to part with their playmate for a while.

"You will not mind if Georgy stays to hear what you have to tell me?" asked Susan. "She knows all about my affairs, as I think you realize."

He nodded, reflecting wryly that evidently she was set on avoiding a tête-à-tête with him. Her manner towards him had undergone a noticeable change. No longer did she blush and stammer when he was by. She regarded him steadily and calmly with her inscrutable dark eyes; and when she spoke to him there was just a trace of reserve in her manner.

"First of all," he said, "I must tell you that your — that is to say, Mrs. Fyfield — was most thankful to get your note. Had you seen her relief when she had read it, I think you would realize that she does indeed hold you in the same affection which she would feel for a niece. She sent you a reply, and here it is." He held out a letter, and Susan took it from him carefully to avoid touching his fingers. "But before you read it," he continued, quickly, "may I tell you of the news she brought back from your old nurse in Islington yesterday?"

Both Susan and Georgiana exclaimed at this, and Susan's face became more animated than before.

"I will spare you all the details that were gone into," he said, dryly. Susan smiled, for she knew only too well how Mrs.

Fyfield would have digressed in telling her tale. "The gist of it was that the woman managed to remember Mr. Watson's abigail saying that they had fetched the child from a village in Middlesex. Half an hour's searching of her memory produced the information that this village had been called Pyncott. I have looked it out, and find that it is a place situated west of Harrow, on the road to the village of Rickmansworth."

"Capital!" cried Georgy, her green eyes glinting. "We must go there at once, and try to find this woman called Polly."

He toyed with his quizzing glass. "I had thought of going there alone."

Both girls raised a quick protest.

"That is just like you, Hugh, to be keeping all the fun to yourself!" exclaimed Georgy in disgust.

"I think I ought to go," put in Susan, with quiet dignity. "There is no reason that I can think of why you should charge yourself with my affairs, sir."

"I offered my help, and you accepted it," he reminded her, gently. "In any event, you will need an escort. Perhaps you might prefer to —" he paused for a moment — "take my brother George?"

"George!" exclaimed Georgy, incredulously. "You must be wanting in your wits Hugh! Take George on an affair of such delicacy! In any case, he is away for a few days, visiting some friends of his who turned up unexpectedly and carried him off."

"In that case perhaps you will allow me to accompany you, Miss Susan?"

Susan looked surprised at the marked diffidence in his tone.

"You are very good, Mr. Eversley," she answered, quietly, "and I should be grateful for your escort."

"Oh, for heaven's sake, stop being polite to each other!" exploded Georgy. "When do we start, Hugh?"

They started off immediately after nuncheon, and by late afternoon had reached a turnpike somewhere along the road to Rickmansworth. At this point, they knew that their road forked; an obliging gatekeeper set them right for Pyncott village.

The road turned out to be nothing better than a rough, waggoners' track, which in any other weather than that of a sunny June day would have been impassable for the Cunningham's delicately sprung coach. As it was, the young ladies received a severe jolting. Georgy wound down the window to call out a protest to her brother, who was riding a little way ahead; but she quickly drew her head in again, because of the dust.

"Phew! What an odiously uneven track this is!" she exclaimed in disgust to Susan. "I dare swear we shall break an axle or something, and then we shall be in a pickle!"

"I suppose this is the only approach to the village," replied Susan, sensibly.

"Well, for my part, I had rather be on horseback. You may depend Hugh had the best of it, as men always contrive to do, my dear!"

At that moment, the coach rounded a bend in the road, and came into a pleasant village of half-timbered cottages which clustered around a small inn. Beau Eversley drew rein, turning his head towards the coach.

"We'll pull in here," he directed, indicating the inn with a gesture of his riding crop.

"Thank goodness for that!" sighed Georgy, as she climbed down from the coach. "Another mile, and there wouldn't have been a whole bone left in our bodies! What say you, Susan?"

But Susan was silent as they made their way to the inn door, narrowly avoiding two or three squawking hens which ran across their path.

Mine host came cheerily forward, though secretly somewhat overawed at the quality of the company which had unexpectedly presented itself at his doors. Most likely it would be visitors for one of the two big houses in the neighbourhood, he told himself, and they would require nothing but to be directed to their destination. This notion was soon dispelled by Beau Eversley's request for a private parlour which might be placed at their disposal. The man's smile broadened as he ushered them into a small, low-ceilinged room which overlooked the road.

"'Tis the public coffee room, y'r honour, but I'll undertake to see that you're not disturbed," he said, wiping with his apron the already well-polished seat of a high-backed settle near the fireplace. "We've got none other — can I bring any refreshment for y'r honour — or the ladies?" He bowed in their direction.

"I think you can," replied the Beau. "And it's not beyond the bounds of possibility that we may require you to furnish us with some kind of dinner, later. Can you manage that?"

The landlord asserted boldly that something could be arranged; and after taking orders for cooling beverages to be brought immediately he retired to review the contents of the larder with his flustered wife.

While the three travellers sipped their drinks, they discussed the best way to set about their mission.

"There are always certain people in a village who can be relied upon to know everyone," stated Hugh. "The innkeeper, the doctor and the clergyman. I doubt if this place is large enough to boast a doctor, and it may not even have a resident clergyman."

"Then that leaves the innkeeper!" exclaimed Georgy, triumphantly. "And I'm sure I don't know why we shouldn't ask him at once."

"One reason," replied her brother, setting down his tankard. "We've no wish to make a stir, and such people gossip."

"Then shall we inquire if there is a clergyman?" asked Susan, diffidently.

This was done; and they were told that the clergyman, a Mr. Robbins, lived hard by the church in a creeper-covered cottage with a chimney that was slightly askew.

"We'll go there immediately," stated Georgy, jumping up.

"Not so fast," drawled Hugh. "For all we know, our friend Mr. Robbins may live alone, and would find it disconcerting, to say the least, to be faced unexpectedly with two young ladies of such undoubted beauty and charm."

Georgiana turned to Susan. "Depend on it, Sue, he's going to suggest something disagreeable — he'd never bother to flatter us so, else!"

Susan dimpled. "I'm entirely of your opinion. All the same, I do think there may be something in what your brother says. Surely we needn't all three go along simply to find out where this woman lives? When we do know that, then perhaps the task of questioning her would be better left in our hands. But I do agree that Mr. Eversley should be the one to approach the clergyman — that is —" she paused, directing a questioning look at Hugh — "if you think so, too, sir?"

He nodded, set down his tankard, and stood up.

"It shouldn't take long. In the meantime, you might care to take up with the landlord the matter of our dinner. We shall certainly be staying."

A few minutes' walk brought him to the cottage. The door was opened by a neat maidservant, who led him through a dim passage into a small, quiet room at the back of the house, where an elderly man sat writing at a small desk in the window. At sight of his visitor, he rose, dismissing the servant with a vague smile. He peered shortsightedly at the visiting card which she had placed in his hand.

"Mr. — er — Eversley," he read, looking up from the card and fixing his visitor with a pair of faded blue eyes. "Please to be seated, sir. A fine, warm afternoon, is it not? Have you come far? Perhaps I can offer you some refreshment?"

Beau Eversley politely declined this offer, and accepted a seat.

"I see you are busy, Mr. Robbins, so I will take up no more of your time than is necessary. I've called on you in the hope that you may be able to assist me in tracing a woman who lives in this village — or perhaps, I should say, who once did so."

A shadow crossed the worn face. "A woman, Mr. — er — Eversley? I trust none of my parishioners is — ah — in any kind of trouble?"

The Beau laughed gently. "Not so far as I know — at any rate, this inquiry does not concern itself with the present day. The woman I am seeking is called Polly, and was resident in this village some fourteen or fifteen years ago."

The old man shook his head. "Polly — it is not uncommon name for a female. And fifteen years since — dear me, it will not be easy. Can you tell me no more, sir?"

The Beau hesitated for a moment, then made up his mind. There should be no fear of gossip here.

"It's difficult, because I myself know so little about her. Only that she lived in this village, and had in her charge at that time a female child who at the age of two or three was removed from her care to that of a relative in London."

A gleam of recognition came into the faded eyes. "Ah, yes, that Polly. To be sure — Polly Whitaker. A godly woman, and a fruitful one, who often acted as wet nurse to the children of the gentlefolk hereabouts."

Beau Eversley's expression sharpened, and he leaned forward eagerly. Mr. Robbins sighed, and shook his head regretfully. "But if you wish to speak with her, sir, I fear you have left it some years too late. Polly Whitaker was interred in our own churchyard four years since come Michaelmas."

Beau Eversley bit back the hasty expression that came to his lips, changing it into a cough.

"That is a pity," he said. "Possibly the unfortunate woman left a husband — or children — who are living here at present?"

"Her husband predeceased her. He was a farm labourer, you know, and succumbed to an inflammation of the lungs, caught during exceptionally severe weather. Only three of her children survived. They are all here in the village, if you should wish to see them."

"Thank you — that is, I wonder if you could tell me what their ages would be?"

"Their ages — dear me, now, let me see." The old man furrowed his brow, and stared through the window with eyes that did not see the buttercup-starred meadows beyond. "It will be in the Parish register, of course —"

"Perhaps I had better give you some idea of what I am looking for," put in Beau Eversley. He hesitated, "Naturally, you would treat as confidential — I just mention it, you know —"

The clergyman inclined his balding head. "Most of my work is confidential, my dear Mr. Eversley. But pray continue. I hope I may be able to help you to whatever it is you wish to discover."

"The fact is, sir, that my interest lies not so much in this Polly herself, but in the child I mentioned just now. A child called Susan, who was taken from the woman's care at about the age of two, and transferred to London. All this happened some fifteen years ago; and unless the woman's own children were old enough at that time to have known anything of Susan which they may still retain, there is no point in my seeking them out."

"I think I can tell you with certainty that they were not, Mr. Eversley; for at the time the eldest of Polly's surviving children cannot have been more than three or four years old himself."

"I see. Thank you, sir." Beau Eversley strove to conceal his inevitable disappointment. "Then there seems no point in my interviewing these people." He paused. "I suppose, Mr. Robbins, you yourself cannot help me? Do you happen to recall anything concerning this child who was called Susan?"

Mr. Robbins slowly shook his shining head with its fringe of thin grey hair.

"I fear not. As is usual with gentlefolk, the ladies of the two important houses in the neighbourhood put out their babies for nursing; and Polly Whitaker was a great favourite with them. For one thing, as I mentioned earlier, she was an exceedingly fruitful woman, and therefore a reliable nurse. I believe also that she was very gentle and patient with little ones. There was often a child from one of the big houses in her care; but I fear, at this distance of time, I cannot clearly recollect any particular child —"

Beau Eversley stood up. "No, sir. Of course it would be too much to expect. But thank you, all the same."

He returned to the inn with lagging step, turning over in his mind what ought to be done next. He might question the innkeeper, of course; but it seemed unlikely that, fifteen years after the event, anyone would remember anything about a small girl who had left the village for good almost as soon as she was able to walk. A neighbour of the late Polly Whitaker's, or a servant from one of the big houses might be able to assist; but there seemed no way of avoiding gossip if such means were to be used.

He was still pondering the question when he walked into the coffee room to find his sister and Susan in animated conversation with the landlord and his wife on the subject of dinner.

"And we can offer you fish from the Pinn, ladies," the innkeeper's wife was assuring them, with a smile.

"The stream over yonder?" asked Susan, waving a hand in the direction of the window. "Can you really catch fish big enough to eat, in that? It looks too shallow."

"'Tis very deep in places, miss, and they catch lovely roach and perch — even a pike, now and then. I mind once, many years agone, it were, when Master Robert from the Place were a little lad — he caught a big 'un, 'e did, durned near as big as hisself, and fell in —"

She broke off, and stared hard at Susan, who was listening to the story with eager dark eyes and parted lips.

"But, bless me!" she continued, her eyes still on Susan's face as though it puzzled her in some way. "You'll know all about that, miss, I'll be bound!"

"I will?" asked Susan, startled. "Why should you say so?"

"Why, you'll be related to them, up at the Place, won't you, miss? It was talking about the fish and that day Master Robert fell in the Pinn — at that moment, you fair put me in mind of him, that you did, though he was fair as fair, and you're dark enough, miss, in all conscience! But it's the expression, see — something in the way you look — I'd know you anywhere for one o' the family, come to think!"

"For one of what family?" asked Beau Eversley, in a more than usually pronounced drawl that served to cover the keen interest he was feeling in the conversation.

"Why, y'r honour, the family up at Pyncott Place, to be sure! Though there's only been the old gentleman living there on his own for many years now, and it's seldom we see any of the rest of the family here in the village to visit him. Not that it's altogether their fault, for they do say that company bain't welcome at the Place these days, unless they'm specially invited. So —"

"Yes, yes, my good woman," interrupted Beau Eversley. "But what is the name of the owner of Pyncott Place?"

"Why, y'r honour, I thought you must know. 'Tis Sir Josiah Radley, to be sure."

Chapter XVI: The Portrait

Pyncott Place was a rambling house that had evidently been started in a modest way in Tudor times, and added to, not altogether harmoniously, by successive generations. A short carriage drive brought Beau Eversley to the porticoed front entrance. His knock was answered by a footman, to whom he handed his card. The man seemed reluctant to admit the visitor; but, as Beau Eversley so evidently expected this, he was at last requested to take a seat in the hall.

It was some time later that a quiet-footed man dressed in a sober suit of grey came to him.

"Mr. Eversley, I believe? Can I be of any service to you, sir?"

Hugh stood up. "I would like to have a word with Sir Josiah Radley, if he can spare me a moment of his time."

The man shook his head. "I fear Sir Josiah is not at liberty to see anyone. But perhaps there is something I can do for you, sir? I am his secretary, and handle all his affairs. My name is East — Matthew East, at your service."

He bowed. Hugh Eversley inclined his head in acknowledgement, and drew his snuff box from his pocket, in order to give himself time to think.

"Perhaps it would be possible for me to arrange an appointment for tomorrow with Sir Josiah? I have come some way in the hope of seeing him personally."

"You will no doubt be aware, Mr. Eversley, that my employer is an old man. He keeps mostly to his room, rarely seeing anyone save his own family, nowadays — and then only by invitation. I am sorry. But, as I mentioned before, I have full authority to attend to all business matters —"

Beau Eversley flicked open the lid of his snuff box, and thoughtfully took a pinch of its contents.

"The matter on which I wish to see your employer would come, I think, more under the heading of a family matter."

Mr. East, the secretary, paused for a moment considering the tall, elegant figure before him. Even in rural Middlesex, the name of Beau Eversley was not unknown. Mr. East was a diplomatic man, and had no wish to give offence to such a one without very good reason.

"In that case of course, Mr. Eversley, it will be suitable for me to approach Sir Josiah on your behalf." There was a door quite close to the spot where they were standing. He moved across, and flung it open. "In the meantime would you care to wait in here, sir? Perhaps I can have some refreshment sent to you?"

Hugh declined this offer, but stepped into the room. "Possibly you should mention to Sir Josiah," he said, as the secretary turned to go, "that I am a close friend of his grandson, Mr. Peter Radley."

Matthew East's expression lightened. "That will certainly be an advantage, Mr. Eversley. You must understand that my employer —" he hesitated a moment — "does not enjoy the kind of health — in short, sir, it is many years since he was in the habit of receiving unexpected visitors. Nowadays such things are apt to put him out."

"I understand perfectly, Mr. East."

The man went, closing the door softly behind him.

Beau Eversley strolled over to the window, and gazed outside with unseeing eyes, turning over in his mind exactly what he would say to Sir Josiah. It would be a ticklish subject to broach, to say the least of it, and supposing they were on the wrong track, after all? Their suspicion was founded on slender enough evidence, for the innkeeper had refused to bear his wife out in thinking that Susan favoured the Radley family in looks: while Hugh himself, who had known Peter and Barbara Radley for many years, could not truthfully say he was able to detect any resemblance. Yet, he thought suddenly, there were times when Susan had reminded him of someone; and had not Horry Walpole commented on that very same thing when they had surprised her lurking in the gardens at Strawberry Hill?

He turned from the window, and glanced idly round the room. A number of portraits hung on the walls. For lack of any better occupation, he moved round and subjected each of them to a cursory scrutiny. There was one of a haughty beauty wearing a green gown with the low, circular décolletage of a hundred years before, that to Beau Eversley's eyes looked hideous. Another showed a gentleman in a flared coat holding a sporting gun in an unlikely attitude. He passed on to the next, a portrait of a boy about twelve years of age who was leaning against a tree, one hand resting on the head of a large dog. He was a handsome child, with a head of very fair curls; but it was not his beauty that suddenly arrested Beau Eversley, making him stare hard at the picture. The eyes were deep and dreamy, the mouth showed the beginnings of a tremulous smile; he knew that expression well, for he had observed it often on a face he was coming to know and love — Susan's face.

He moved closer to the picture, hoping to read at its foot the name of the subject. After a moment, he drew back, disappointed, for only the artist's name appeared. He looked once more into the painted brown eyes which were so like the dark ones; which now had the power to touch his heart.

He controlled a quiet start as he heard the opening door behind him. Matthew East entered quietly.

"I'm afraid I have been unable to prevail upon Sir Josiah to see you, sir. I am sorry; I did all that was possible, but he is quite adamant."

Beau Eversley turned. "I see," he replied. "Is there any possibility of making another appointment?"

Mr. East shook his head. "I fear not. My employer — ah — made it quite clear that he did not wish to see you, sir, at any time."

Beau Eversley raised one eyebrow. "In spite of the fact that I wish to discuss a family matter with him?"

The secretary hesitated. "Shall we perhaps say — because of that, Mr. Eversley? My employer's relations with his family are somewhat — um — ah — unusual, sir."

"I see." Beau Eversley idly lifted his quizzing glass and levelled it at the portrait which had so attracted him. "That picture, Mr. East — can you tell me who is the subject?"

The secretary followed his gaze. "That is a likeness of Mr. Robert Radley, taken when he was a boy. As you are acquainted with the family, sir, you will doubtless be aware that he was the younger son of my employer, and died, when quite a young man — I believe in his early twenties."

Beau Eversley nodded. "I have certainly heard something to that effect. That would be well before your time, Mr. East, I imagine?"

"Indeed, yes, Mr. Eversley. I have been in Sir Josiah's service only for the last twelve years."

"Quite a spell, nevertheless," replied Hugh, in a casual tone. "Well, it is evident that I can do no good here, so I'll take my leave. I must thank you, Mr. East, for your endeavours on my behalf. I'm very grateful indeed to you. Good day."

He was turning out of the carriage drive into the lane which led back to the inn, when two figures in pale shades of muslin swooped down on him, breaking into his thoughts with eager questions.

"We simply couldn't wait for you to return!" exclaimed Georgy. "We had to know at once! Besides, it will be difficult for us to talk much over dinner, for the inn servants will be coming and going all the time. How did you go on, Hugh? Did you see him? What did he say?"

"Did you discover anything?" echoed Susan, anxiously watching his face.

He gallantly offered each of them an arm before attempting to answer. Susan accepted after a barely perceptible hesitation, lightly resting her hand on the sleeve of his dark green riding coat, but keeping her distance from his side.

"In a sense," he began, "I achieved nothing." He recounted briefly what had passed between himself and Mr. East. "But yet we may say," he finished, "that I did not entirely waste my time — or should I say *our* time? — in visiting Pyncott Place." He turned towards Susan. "There is a portrait hanging in a room there, which bears a striking resemblance to you, Miss Susan. This in spite of the fact that the subject is just as fair as you are dark."

Georgy exclaimed in delight, but her brother ignored her. His eyes were on Susan. She raised her face to his, and as their eyes met, he felt his pulses quicken.

"Is it — the person mentioned by the landlady of the Black Horse? Is it — Robert Radley?"

He nodded. "The same. It's a painting of him as a young boy. That makes it easier to trace a likeness to a female than would have been the case if the portrait had been of Robert Radley as a man! It was talking of the boy, you may remember, that made the innkeeper's wife detect a likeness between you."

"Who would Robert Radley be?" asked Georgiana. "He's not Barbara's father, I know, and I've never heard her mention an uncle."

"Yet there was an uncle — a younger brother — who died as a young man, and about whom there seems to be some kind of mystery," replied Hugh.

"Surely you must know all about him, Hugh, for you and Peter were at school together," said Georgy impatiently.

"My dear sister, do you suppose that schoolboys spend their time discussing their relatives?" he retorted with scorn. "Let me tell you, you're very wide of the mark, if you do."

"Oh, I don't see why not. I told Susan everything about you — didn't I, Sue?"

"What a bore she must have found you!" said Hugh, quickly, before Susan was obliged to reply. "Well, the only time I ever heard Peter mention his uncle was certainly not at school, but quite recently; when he explained to me that his grandfather's irascible disposition had something to do with Robert Radley's death. But exactly what, I can't say, though I did gain some impression of a skeleton in the family cupboard."

"Well, there you are, then!" exclaimed Georgy, triumphantly. "You have only to ask Peter to tell you all about it —"

"It is, of course," he said, mockingly, "a simple matter to ask a man to reveal to you the seamier side of his family affairs."

Before Georgiana could reply to this, Susan suddenly pulled her arm away from Hugh's, and went running ahead down the lane.

The others stood still for a moment, staring after her. "Come back, Susan!" called Georgy. "What in the world are you doing?"

The Beau dropped his sister's arm, and caught up with Susan in a few quick strides. He took her arm in a gently restraining grasp.

"Susan —"

At that, she turned to face him, and he was shocked to see the tears running freely down her face. Acting on impulse, he placed an arm protectively about her, and tenderly wiped away the tears with a handkerchief which he had drawn from his pocket.

"Susan — my little love —" The words were drawn involuntarily from him.

Afterwards, he reflected that perhaps it was as well that Georgy had come up with them at that very moment, and had herself taken over the comforting of Susan.

He drew a little away from the girls, watching them. Presently, Susan disengaged herself from Georgy's embrace, rubbed her eyes fiercely with the borrowed handkerchief, and swallowed hard once or twice.

"Of course, I kn-know that I am s-silly," she gulped. "But you were joking about skeletons in the cupboard, and all the time it was plain to see that you thought —"

She turned suddenly on Hugh.

"You believe that Robert Radley is — was — my father, don't you?"

"It certainly begins to look very like it," he answered.

"Then — then that would make me —" She fought bravely to control the trembling of her lips.

"But, Susan, there's no need to put yourself in a taking even if you are this Robert Radley's natural daughter!" stated the forthright Georgiana. "Your father was a gentleman — what matter if he did not wed your mother? And it might even turn out," she added, thoughtfully, "that she was a female of good family, too. She might have been some other man's wife, and formed a — a — an indiscreet liaison with Robert Radley. Yes!" she exclaimed, triumphantly. "And that would account, you know, for the circumstances of your upbringing! Naturally she dare not disclose the truth to her husband, and so she had you adopted!"

It crossed Beau Eversley's mind that in such circumstances it was more usual for the erring lady to pass off the child as her husband's. Considering the sex and youth of his audience, he suppressed the remark, merely saying, "Possibly. But I think we are taking too much for granted at present. If it should turn out that Susan is Robert Radley's daughter, so much the better. We must not jump to conclusions however. A resemblance to a painting — however marked — is insufficient evidence. The question is, where to get proof positive of our suspicions?"

"I still think Peter is the person to ask!" insisted Georgy. "Oh, yes, I know you gentlemen never pry into each other's private affairs, however close your friendship is — but there must be ways in which you could work the conversation round to the subject. I am sure I could do it. Oh, Hugh!" Her face lit up, as a fresh idea occurred to her. "Do you think I could ask Barbara? Just casually, you know — I swear I wouldn't give her any notion of why I was curious!"

"Perhaps not, though I wouldn't care to wager on that," replied her brother, cynically. "But at all costs Susan must be protected from gossip, so the fewer people we approach, the better. No, leave it to me. I'll try my luck with Peter."

He turned to Susan, and once more drew her arm within his.

"And now if we may," he said, smiling into her still sombre eyes, "let us return to the Black Horse. Young ladies may manage to keep going tolerably well on fresh air, but the average man at this time of day finds his thoughts turning irresistibly toward his dinner."

Beau Eversley returned to London the afternoon of the following day. He was accompanied by his brother George, who had put in an appearance at Richmond early that same morning.

George made no secret of his reluctance to leave Susan's side.

"I don't want to go back to Town above half," he said, keeping her hand in his while they said good-bye. "But I must put myself in funds again, and it keeps the old man sweet if I turn up every so often." He gazed into her eyes with an expression that reminded Beau Eversley of an ailing spaniel. "D'you mean to stay much longer here with my sister Eve? If so, I'll be back again before long, see if I'm not."

"I can't say," replied Susan, gently withdrawing her hand from his ardent grasp, and offering it to his brother with a cool smile. "I know Georgy's impatient to be gone, so possibly we may both be back in London in a day or two."

Hugh bowed low over her hand, but did not retain it one moment longer than was strictly proper.

Georgiana watched him approvingly. He really was complete to a touch, was Hugh; no wonder they called him Beau Eversley. Not for him the callow tactics of his younger brother — Beau Eversley's pursuit of a female was a pleasure to watch. She frowned suddenly, wondering just how serious they were, either George or Hugh. Of course, with George it was calf-love; but that could grow and strengthen with time. As for Hugh — her frown deepened as she tried to fathom Hugh.

"Did you mean what you said?" she asked Susan, as soon as they were alone. "About returning to Town, I mean."

Susan nodded. "Yes, I —" she hesitated — "I believe I could return now, in spite of the fact that I still do not know for certain who I am. But I can't run away for ever, can I? Some time I will have to go back and face things as they are." She sighed. "All the same, I don't feel quite as desperate as I did on that dreadful evening when I came to you for help. I felt then that I simply had to escape from it all — from my aunt, who wasn't really my aunt, and Cynthia, who wasn't really my cousin, and — and —"

"And Beau Eversley," put in Georgy, giving her a shrewd look, "who wasn't really your betrothed."

"Yes," acknowledged Susan, with a faint blush. "Everyone — and everything."

"You don't mind now, do you? About Hugh, I mean? You've quite go over your *tendre* for him, haven't you?"

Susan looked at her friend for a moment in silence.

"What makes you say that?" she asked at last.

"Oh, it's as plain as can be!" replied Georgy. "You no longer gaze at him in the moonstruck way you used to —"

"Did I do *that*?" demanded Susan, in horror.

Georgiana laughed. "To be sure you did!" she insisted, heartlessly. "Cheer up — I dare say *he* may not have noticed — but I must say it was obvious to any other female."

"Oh, dear!" Susan hung her head.

"Well, as I said, he may not have noticed, so there's no need to go into a decline about it. Besides nothing could be more changed than your manner towards him now — if he ever had any notion that you were enamoured of him, he must be quite disillusioned, I assure you."

"You find my manner so very different?"

"Decidedly! And I fancy I know why." Georgiana stole a sly look at Susan's thoughtful face. "You and my brother George are getting on delightfully together, are you not? All the Eversley men are acknowledged to be handsome — of course, George has not quite Hugh's style and address, but he will be presentable enough in another year or two — and it will be quite that before you can be wed, my dear, so you don't need to worry."

Susan put up her hands to her cheek, which had suddenly grown warm.

"Georgiana! What nonsense are you talking?"

"Oh, come, you can't gull me, Sue! I've watched you at close quarters for the last fortnight, and I assure you I never saw George more taken with anyone in his life! Come to think of it," she added fair-mindedly, "I couldn't have done, for he's never shown even the remotest interest in any female before. It's a pity he must return to Town; but he's bound to show himself at home for a bit, you know."

"It's most likely," remarked Susan, in a flat voice, "that I shall never marry."

"Stuff! I'll wager you'll marry George when he comes of age, and has control of his own fortune. And of course I'll be your bridesmaid — and what shall I wear? I think perhaps blue —"

In spite of herself, Susan burst into laughter. "Oh, Georgy! You are such a — such an idiot, my love! I dare say," she added sobering, "you'll be wed long before I am — in fact I know it. Who do you suppose would want to marry a girl without a name?"

"Long before then, you may have found your name," insisted Georgy, stubbornly. "And even if you haven't why cannot you go on being Mrs. Fyfield's niece, just as you believed yourself to be in the past? Only a few of us will know your secret, and I swear we will keep it to the death!"

She struck a melodramatic attitude, and once more Susan could not help laughing. "That's all very well, Georgy," she said, after a moment, "but now I've learnt so much I can't rest until I know the whole truth."

"I have no doubt in my own mind that Robert Radley was your father," insisted Georgiana.

"But as your brother said," objected Susan, "there's no real proof as yet —"

"Pooh! Gentlemen are so prosy, my dear, always wanting to prove everything! I think a female can often rely on her intuition, and mine tells me indisputably that you are Robert Radley's child."

"Well if that is so," demurred Susan, "I am most likely illegitimate. What does your intuition make of that?"

"What if you are? You wouldn't be the first, I assure you; and no one would think any the worse of you for it, providing your father was a gentleman."

"But suppose he was not?"

"I tell you I'm certain he was. Besides," added Georgy, "you've no need to tell anyone, even if things don't turn out as we expect. As I said before, you are still Mrs. Fyfield's niece in the eyes of the world; and the only people who know differently would never betray you."

"But it would mean —" began Susan, then stopped suddenly. "Oh, never mind! The fact is, I do feel a deal better about everything than I did when I came to you on that dreadful evening; and I'd like you to know how very grateful I am to you, Georgy — in fact to all your family — for your kindness to me."

"Silly, you don't need to thank me! You know how we've always helped each other out of scrapes, you and I! As for the others — well, Eve told me that she is very fond of you, Susan;

and George, as we both know, is absolutely head over ears as far as you are concerned! I say, though, Sue!" She broke off, and gave an impish chuckle. "Do you know, I believe Hugh has actually taken one of his fancies to you! I don't know if you've noticed anything, but I noticed it first on that day he came to Richmond seeking you. Since then there have been several little incidents — I can't mistake, for I've seen him so often like this with other females! There was Bar—" she broke off, abruptly. "Oh, well, never mind that! The only thing is, though," she added, regretfully, "it never lasts with him for long — I know that, too! So it's a good thing that you've quite got over your former feelings for him, you can see."

"Yes," replied Susan, expressionlessly. "Yes, I suppose it is."

"All the same, my dear," summed up Georgy, reflectively, "it's a feather in your cap."

Chapter XVII: An Expert in Scandal

Beau Eversley had been back in Town for several days before he found any opportunity of a private conversation with his friend Peter Radley. Even then, it was in Whites Club, during a lull when neither man happened to be at play. At first, it looked as though they were to talk of nothing but their luck; after a lengthy inquest on the game they had just quitted, Hugh ostentatiously stifled a yawn, and tried to turn the conversation into more promising channels.

"Do you mean to take a house in Brighton this year?" he asked.

Peter shrugged. "Haven't made up my mind yet. Either that, or the country — must get out of Town presently, I suppose, like everyone else. Do you go to Brighton, then?"

The Beau shook his head. "I don't think so. I'm fixed here at present."

"The McCann?" queried Peter with a grin — "I hear she's giving a Farewell Performance soon, and leaving Town for good. Wonder where she's going — more important, who is to accompany her? Not that I mean to pry, old chap," he added, the grin broadening.

"You are perfectly at liberty, of course," drawled Hugh, "to draw any conclusions you choose, however erroneous." He drew out his snuff box, offering it to Peter. "Where do you go in the country — to your grandfather's place?"

Peter paused in the act of accepting a pinch of snuff, and cast a startled look at his friend. "Good God, no! Whatever put such a fiendish notion into your head! Never go there if I can possibly avoid it; no man in his right mind would ever seek my grandfather's company."

"I seem to remember," replied Hugh, carelessly, "that you once mentioned Sir Josiah was possessed of an uncertain temper."

"Uncertain temper! My dear fellow, the old man's a regular fiend, I assure you! Don't envy my sister Babs — she's obliged to go down there with my mother in a day or two, to break the news."

"News?"

"Warburton's come up to scratch, and offered for her. Been accepted, too — subject to that old devil's approval, as all our family arrangements are."

"Then it would perhaps be a trifle premature to wish your sister happy, at present?"

"It certainly would. Old Josh is quite capable of saying Warburton won't do, just to satisfy some devilish whim of his own. No saying which way the cat'll jump, where he's concerned."

"Odd," said Hugh, devoting a great deal of attention to the business of returning the snuff box to his pocket. "I believe you once said that your grandfather's contrary disposition owed something to the untimely death of your father's younger brother, Robert Radley?"

"So I've heard my father say," replied Peter. "I say, Hugh, what mixture is this? I like it better than any I've tried so far. Would you care to try a pinch of mine, and give me your opinion of it?"

He started to produce his own snuff box, but the Beau stopped him with a gesture. The last thing he wanted at present was a turn in the conversation.

"It's my own mixture," he said, quickly. "I'll let you into the secret next time you're at my house. But, tell me, what caused your uncle's death?"

Peter wrinkled his brow. "Dashed if I know — it was an accident," he replied, after a moment. "But there's more to it than that, I fancy. Tell you the truth, I've never really known the whole story — I was only a youngster, of course, and away at school into the bargain when it happened; and whenever I've chanced to ask about it since, my parents have shut me up pretty damn quick. Some kind of scandal, I suppose. Even the best families have 'em. But I hope Old Josh won't take it out on Babs, for she's set on Warburton, right enough. Funny, when you think of it —" he finished, with a sidelong glance at his friend — "for at one time, she had very different notions." He pushed away his chair, and stood up. "Oh, well, no accounting for such things. Might as well see if we can get another game, I suppose. Coming?"

At the time of this conversation Susan herself was already back in London. Shortly after Beau Eversley's visit to Richmond, Evelina's husband had returned from his travels. This lent force to Georgy's persuasions that it was time for herself and Susan to leave for home. Happy in the reunion with her husband, Eve did not press them too hard to stay, but was quick to offer Susan a welcome at any time she chose to return.

Susan wished that she could have felt as certain of her welcome in Duke Street. But she need not have concerned herself: Mrs. Fyfield's reception of her charge was all that she could have wished — less casual than that given her in the past on her return from school for the holidays, yet not so fussy as to seem insincere. Behind it, she sensed a genuine affection which both surprised and pleased her. At first, she stumbled over saying Mrs. Fyfield's name, uncertain how to address the woman who she had always thought of as her aunt.

"Aunt Hattie will do," pronounced that lady, firmly. "I've always been Aunt Hattie, and it's too late now to change. Besides, my dear, I've long since accepted you as my very own niece. After Cynthia is wed, you and I may go on very comfortably, here together, I am sure, until someone comes along to marry you, in your turn — whether Beau Eversley," she finished, giving Susan a keen look, "or another — it makes no odds."

Cynthia, who was on her way out of the room at the time, paused on hearing this remark.

"Beau Eversley, indeed!" she said, with a smirk. "I hope you don't imagine, Susan, that he has been wearing the willow for you while you've been away! I have it on very good authority that he's been seen everywhere with that Irish play actress. They say he can't bear to be out of her sight for half a day!"

The door closed behind her.

"Pay no heed to her!" advised Mrs. Fyfield. "She's as high-strung as a racehorse at present! But no wonder — we poor females are all the same when we're about to tie the knot! You'll know what it is, my dear, when your turn comes, presently."

Susan shook her head. "Who would be likely to want to marry me, now?" she said, bitterly.

"Fustian! Don't be indulging in such morbid thoughts, child! I'm sure I know of no reason why anyone should not. You're as pretty as paint, besides being less spoilt than some of these acknowledged Beauties who carry the Town by storm. But tell me, Susan —" she broke off, as a fresh thought occurred to her — "have you heard anything from Mr. Eversley about the search he was going to make for that nursemaid called Polly?

I've been looking out for him every day in the hope of hearing some news."

Susan told her about the journey into Middlesex, and the conclusions which they had drawn from it.

"The Radleys!" exclaimed Mrs. Fyfield in surprise. "So it seems likely you are related to them! Well, if so, child, you have nothing to fear from the world if the whole business were to be made public at once!"

"Oh, Aunt Hattie, promise you won't say a word?" begged Susan, earnestly. "Not even to Cynthia! It's by no means certain — in fact Mr. Eversley said that there was nothing at all one could call proof — and it would be dreadful if it should all be a mistake, and any rumour came to their ears!"

"You know me, Susan," replied Mrs. Fyfield, with dignity. "Did I not keep the whole thing secret for all those years? But it's not going to be a simple matter," she added, thoughtfully, "for anyone to obtain conclusive proof. Beau Eversley is, of course, a great friend of the family —"

"He means to try and find out for me," said Susan. "But supposing he can't? As he says, it's not an easy matter to ask intimate questions, even of very old friends. And where will I be if he can discover nothing to the purpose? For there seems no other way of finding out about my parentage."

"You'll be exactly where you are at present," replied Mrs. Fyfield, with energy, "and there's nothing wrong with that. No one need know you are not my niece, unless you choose to tell them so."

"That's what Georgy said —"

"Yes, well, for once she showed great good sense — though in general I think her a bit wild, although you may not like to hear it, for she *has* been a very good friend to you, I know. Very good sense," she repeated, firmly. "And when it comes to marriage, why, you have all that money, you know. So that even if being my niece is not exactly the strongest recommendation — though nothing to be ashamed of, mark you, for both your uncle's family (Oh dear, there I go again! I can't remember that you are not truly my niece!) both his family, as I was saying, and my own, were gentlefolk, though not highly connected —" She stopped, and took a deep breath. "Oh, dear, where was I? I have forgot. But what it comes to, dearest child, is that you can marry anyone who asks you, and with a clear conscience, without troubling your head further about your parentage."

Susan could not agree with this, but she refrained from further argument. The whole household was at present plunged into feverish activity, for the date of Cynthia's wedding was now fixed, and in Mrs. Fyfield's words, there were a thousand things to do. Most of these took Cynthia and her mother out of the house, so that Susan found herself alone a good deal. She could, of course, have accompanied the others on their trips to the various establishments which were to furnish Cynthia with her trousseau; but most often she declined, preferring to remain at home.

On one of these occasions, Beau Eversley called.

"Forgive me for disturbing you," he said, bowing. "I thought to find Mrs. Fyfield with you."

Susan offered him her hand; smiling in a composed way that was in marked contrast, he thought suddenly, to the confusion she had once shown whenever he confronted her. Her manner, however, was completely natural.

"Have you news for me?" she asked, eagerly. "Oh — I beg your pardon — won't you sit down?"

He did so, watching while she settled herself against the arm of a striped satin sofa. She cupped her pointed chin in her hand, and a dark ringlet fell against her neck, just touching the tiny blue frill which edged her dress. That gesture reminded him of someone, he thought suddenly. Who could it be? Was it Barbara Radley?

She lowered her eyes, and he realized that he had been staring at her for several minutes.

"I fear I must disappoint you," he said, making an effort to concentrate. "I haven't succeeded in finding out anything conclusive. What Radley says makes it certain that there was some kind of —" he paused, rejecting the word "scandal" and casting about for a less offensive one — "of incident in which Robert Radley was involved immediately before his sudden death. The difficulty is that Peter can give me no details, because it is a subject which his parents have always refused to discuss with him."

"I see," she said, thoughtfully. Her dark eyes met his, and he steeled himself to keep back the warmth which suddenly flooded his own. Everything about her — every movement, every gesture, even the tones of her voice — now seemed to have the power to play upon his senses as though an expert hand touched a delicately tuned musical instrument. It had been like this before, he reminded himself, often and often. Desire was no new sensation to Beau Eversley; but with this girl there was something added...

"So now there is no hope of ever discovering who I am?" she continued. Her voice was quiet, but wistful. "I suppose it's just as Georgy and Aunt Hattie say — it doesn't really matter; no one else need ever know that I'm not the person I seem to be."

"Susan!" He leaned forward impetuously, as if about to take her hand. She changed position, suddenly sitting upright with hands clasped tightly together in her lap.

"Yes?" she said, in a thin voice.

He drew back. "Nothing. That is — I was about to agree with what you had just said." He stood up, and took a turn or two about the room, trying to keep his eyes off her. "It does not really matter to anyone but yourself. Where you are known, you must always be — highly valued — on your own merits."

"Thank you." For a moment, she felt a lump in her throat, but she swallowed resolutely. "You are very good. All the same —" she paused, and shook her head sadly. "I would like to know," she concluded.

"You shall. I will think of a way." He stopped pacing and turned to face her. He was in control again now, as the drawl in his voice clearly showed. "But let's forget it just for a little while." He glanced out of the window. "It's a lovely morning. Can I persuade you to come driving in the Park with me?"

She began a reply, but was interrupted by a knock on the door. The shabby footman entered to announce another visitor.

"George!" exclaimed Susan, in relief, springing up from the sofa. "By all means show him in!"

A moment later, George entered the room resplendent in a yellow and white striped waistcoat and with his cravat tied in a new and dashing style. Beau Eversley's eyeglass went up, and he nodded sagely.

"What the devil are you doing here, Hugh?" George's face changed on seeing his brother.

"I might ask you the same question, my dear chap," drawled the Beau.

"Well, if you must know, I've called in to see if Miss Fyfield will honour me by letting me take her for a spin in the Park," replied George, a little on the defensive. "Not that it's any concern of yours, of course."

"Now isn't that odd?"

"Odd? What d'ye mean, odd?" asked George, suspiciously.

"Don't you mean to shake hands with me?" put in Susan, uncertain where this brotherly exchange was leading.

"You bet I do," said George, wholeheartedly, taking her hand in a warm clasp, and bowing — "How d'ye do, Susan? How delightful to see you again! You don't want this fellow here, do you? Shall I turn him out for you?"

"You are welcome to try, dear boy," replied the Beau, in a languid tone.

"If you fancy I —"

"Don't be absurd George," said Susan, laughing. "Your brother was just leaving when you arrived, I believe."

"Was I?" Hugh studied her face gravely for a moment. "Yes, perhaps I was. I trust you will enjoy your drive in the Park. As for the other matter, do not let it concern you. Please present my compliments to Mrs. Fyfield, and say I am sorry to have missed her. Your servant, ma'am."

His fingers touched hers briefly; he bowed, and was gone.

He had almost reached his own house before his pulse was quite steady again.

Once indoors, he settled himself in the library with the intention of attending to some correspondence. He found himself unable to concentrate, however, and sat staring at a blank sheet of paper, while thoughts chased round in his mind. He wondered how long his present feeling for Susan might last. Was it only infatuation? If so, no doubt it would not long survive her present obvious indifference. The way she had jumped up when George was announced...

He set his jaw firmly. It would be a very good thing for them both if they were to become attached to each other. Of course, there could be no thought of marriage with George still at

Oxford and not in command of his own means. But this was all to the good. Another few years should give George the added maturity needed to make him a good husband; while, as for Susan, she was young enough to wait. He wondered how deep the attraction between them was already. He recognized in his brother all the symptoms of calf-love common to young men of his age who had never been much in the petticoat line. Such a feeling could die out as quickly as Susan's hero worship of himself had done; on the other hand, it could sometimes grow into a lasting attachment.

Suddenly he threw down his pen, and rose impatiently from the desk. To hell with everything! He wished he had never met the girl — never gone that day to Strawberry Hill.

He pulled his thoughts up short for the moment. Strawberry Hill! Why had it never struck him before? That was where he must go to find an answer to Susan's puzzle! If there was one man in the whole of England who would know the full story of any Society scandal, that man was surely Horace Walpole.

Chapter XVIII: The Lion's Den

"What d'you say?" asked George, eagerly. "Will you come?"

Susan pulled herself back from an immense distance. "Mm? Oh — oh, yes, I suppose so."

"Well, I must say," protested George in a hurt tone, "you might sound a bit more enthusiastic about it. What's amiss? Don't you wish to come out with me?"

"Oh, I beg your pardon!" She flashed a smile of great sweetness at him. "Of course I would like it of all things! And it is so good of you to offer."

"I don't know," replied George, looking a little pink. "The fact is I'd do a great deal for you, Susan."

"Would you?" She regarded him thoughtfully for a moment, as though weighing something in her mind.

"Yes, I dashed well would. In fact," he added, thinking this needed improving upon, "you've only to name anything you'd like me to do for you, and it's as good as done."

"Anything?"

He hesitated for a fraction of a second. "Well — anything within reason, that is."

"Oh!" she drew back, as though disappointed. "Then it's no use asking you the thing that was in my mind."

"You mean there's something you'd like me to do?" he asked incredulously.

She nodded. "Yes. But I'm not sure you would consider it a reasonable request."

"We'll see about that. Just tell me what it is, first."

"Very well." She took a deep breath. "George, instead of driving me in the Park, I want you to take me to a village in Middlesex."

"Middlesex?" he stared. "Whatever for?"

"I can't tell you — that's another thing you'll have to do for me — trust me."

"That's all very well," he demurred, common sense reasserting itself, "but it's a bit of a queer start, ain't it? Besides, I couldn't drive you all the way to Middlesex in a curricle. Wouldn't be proper. Driving in the Park's one thing —"

"Oh, very well," replied Susan, coldly. "But I *thought* you said you'd do *anything* —"

She watched him struggle for a moment in silence.

"All right, you win," he conceded. "I'll take you; but tell you what — I think we ought to take Georgy along with us. There might be a bit of a kick up if we went alone. We can't all go in the curricle, of course," he added, as an afterthought. "We'll get another vehicle for you two and I'll ride. What about your aunt? Will she let you go, d'you think?"

"I shan't ask her," said Susan, quickly. "There isn't time, for I don't know when she and Cynthia may return home. I'll leave a message for her. Very well, we can take Georgy, if you think it's best. But *do* let us go — now, please."

But when they reached the house, Georgy was out with Lady Eversley, and was not expected back for some hours. An argument ensued, which Susan ended by stating defiantly that she would go alone if George did not care to take her.

"I really believe you would!" he said, with reluctant admiration. "You don't care a fig for the conventions, do you?"

"Well, if *I* don't, I can't see why you should!" retorted Susan.

"Different thing altogether, my dear girl," George began to explain. "I'm in a deuced awkward position, don't you see? Kind of responsible for you, if you know what I mean."

"No," said Susan flatly. "I don't know. No one's responsible for me but myself." She broke off, and added in a quieter tone — "I'm entirely on my own. Anyway —" her voice quickened again — "for goodness' sake do let's stop arguing, and go."

So they went in the curricle. After they had left behind London's traffic and were bowling along in the country, George tried to question Susan about her reasons for the journey, but she was resolute in refusing to answer him. He protested that she ought to realize she could trust him; adding in a slightly injured tone that he was quite sure she had kept secrets from him when she had been staying in Richmond, but that she had seemed ready enough to share them with the rest of his family.

"I suppose you put me down as a gabster!" he contended, indignantly. "And there's an end of it!"

Susan laid a hand placatingly on his arm.

"Dear, kind George," she pleaded, "if only you will not tease me now! Perhaps later I may be able to tell you the whole — only there is something I must find out first, and that is why we must go to Pyncott."

He was very willing to be cajoled by her, and so he dropped the subject, confining his conversation to the sights and incidents of the road. Apart from a slight altercation with a wagoner, who for some time refused to pull in to the hedge sufficiently to allow George to pass, these were unexciting. Not far from Edgware, George felt the pangs of thirst, and suggested that they might stop and refresh themselves at the next village inn. Susan insisted, however, that they must press on; she felt too nervous to bear any delay in putting her desperate plan into action. She dared not think what George's reactions would be when she told him what she intended to do.

They were both feeling a trifle jaded by the time they turned off the turnpike road along the carters' track that led to the village of Pyncott. The horses, too, were flagging.

"It's the heat —" began George, then broke off as the roughness of the track set every tooth in his head chattering. "My God, Susan, where in thunder have you brought us to? Damme if I ever drove over such a surface!"

"It's all right," Susan assured him, clinging on to the seat for dear life. "We're nearly there now — there's an inn just a little further along, where we may halt."

"So I should hope — hold tight!"

He flung himself protectively against her as the vehicle gave a shuddering lurch, and came to an abrupt standstill. It rocked for a moment as though it would topple over, while George held firmly on to the reins, and Susan clung just as firmly to George. After a few moments it subsided, remaining upright as if by a miracle.

"Phew!" exclaimed George, then added "My God!" for good measure.

"What — what happened?" stammered Susan, still clinging to him.

"Orlando stumbled. Can't wonder at it. Here, take the reins for a minute, while I get down and take a look at him," ordered George, brusquely.

Susan obeyed with some misgivings. George leapt from the curricle, and, going to the frightened horses, managed at last to quieten them. Then he bent to examine the outside horse, Orlando.

After a moment, he led both animals forward a few paces. He swore softly.

"Orlando's limping," he said, anxiously. "I only hope he may not have strained a tendon. Hell and the devil! Why did we have to come along this cursed track? How far's this inn of yours?"

"It's only just round the bend," said Susan, in contrite tones. "George, I am so sorry! Shall I get out?"

"No point in that," replied her escort, shortly. "We can't leave the damned curricle stuck here in the middle of the road, so I'll have to risk walking him as far as the inn, that's all. You stay there and just hold the reins."

He had some difficulty in persuading the injured Orlando to move; but, once this was done, the equipage made its halting progress to the Black Horse.

"Let's hope there'll be someone here who knows enough about horses not to make the poor old fellow a cripple for life," said George, bitterly, as they drew into the forecourt of the inn. "I suppose it serves me right for not bringing my own groom with me, but I didn't want to make a stir about you and I going off like this, and even the best servants will gossip."

Susan apologized in a small voice, feeling responsible for the accident. Her escort did not seem very ready to reassure her. The truth was that until recently, George's horses had been the ruling passion of his life. At present his anxiety for Orlando outweighed all other considerations, as Susan could very well see.

She wondered if he was beginning to regret having brought her here, and her feelings of guilt increased. She had to acknowledge that she had certainly played upon his feelings for herself in persuading him to make the journey. It was not the kind of thing she had liked to do, but at the time she could think of no other way of accomplishing what mattered to her so desperately. And now, if she had caused permanent injury to one of his favourite horses, she felt that she could never forgive herself.

Susan was quickly recognized by the landlord of the inn, and every attention was given to the visitors. George lost no time in seeking expert aid for Orlando, and was lucky enough to find that the landlord knew the very man to help in this way. While refreshment was served to the hot and dusty travellers, an ostler was sent in search of him. George quickly tossed off a tankard of cool ale, and, with a hurried excuse to Susan, made off in the direction of the stables.

For some time, Susan sat alone in the coffee room, inwardly restive at the delay in carrying out her plan. She had meant to confide in George, and enlist his aid in getting unseen into Pyncott Place. Now she must wait until the horse had been attended to; and by that time George might not be in a mood to help her with so unconventional a scheme. It was already over four hours since she had first embarked on her enterprise, for time had been wasted in calling on Georgiana in the hope of bringing her with them. Now this further delay looked like prolonging the venture, making it doubtful if she and George could reach home before nightfall. And if they did not — Susan's heart contracted as she thought of all the possible complications to her situation.

There was nothing else for it. She must go to Pyncott Place alone. George would be safely occupied in the stables for the next hour or two, and would most likely never even notice her absence. All the same, she gave the landlord a message for him to the effect that she was just taking a stroll about the village.

She drew on her gloves, and left the inn, walking purposefully in the direction of Pyncott Place.

When she reached the gates to the house, she hesitated, casting a thoughtful look along the drive. She tried the gate. The latch yielded to her touch, but in spite of this, she drew back. To enter by the front way would not serve her purpose. Like Beau Eversley, she would be met by Sir Josiah's secretary, and politely turned away. She must find some way of coming face to face with the formidable Sir Josiah himself.

She walked some distance round the boundary wall in search of another gate which might lead to the back quarters of the house. After a time she found one, and thankfully tried it. To her chagrin, she discovered that it was locked.

She stood still for a while, considering what to do.

It was then that she heard the clopping of a horse's hoofs over the turf. She turned her head in the direction of the sound, and saw that the approaching rider was a female in an expensively cut habit of dark blue cloth, with a jaunty, feathered cap of the same colour set over her ringlets of bright gold. Susan's heart missed a beat This was none other than Barbara Radley.

She thought rapidly. Miss Radley must be here on a visit to her grandfather. Ready to clutch at straws, Susan saw that here might be a way of gaining access to Sir Josiah. Without pausing to remember that Barbara had met her only once at Georgiana's party, and might not even recognize her, Susan gave the rider a cheery greeting.

Barbara looked puzzled for a moment as she reined in her horse. Then her face cleared.

"Oh, of course, you are a friend of Georgiana Eversley's, are you not? We met at her party, I believe, Miss — er —"

She hesitated, evidently unable to recall Susan's name. Susan quickly supplied the deficiency.

"Yes, of course," replied Barbara, dismounting. "How stupid of me to forget!" She offered her hand. "I am on a short visit to my grandfather at present — he lives in the house yonder — Pyncott Place."

"Yes, I know." Susan drew a deep breath, and began to speak quickly, before her courage should desert her. "Miss Radley, I dare say you may think it very odd of me to ask this, but I assure you I have a very particular, most pressing reason for my request — I must see your grandfather at once. Do you think you could possibly take me to him?"

Barbara's lovely blue eyes opened wide, and her lips parted slightly. "But — but why do you not ask for him at the house?" she stammered.

"Because it's no good. He doesn't know me."

Barbara stared as though she had some doubts about Susan's sanity. "Doesn't know you? Then why —"

"I told you that you'd think it odd — I can't explain yet — perhaps not ever. But oh, please do help me!" Susan laid a hand on the other girl's arm and turned pleading dark eyes up to her face. "I know your grandfather's secretary will turn me away at once, because I cannot tell him what my business is. Even if you are so good as to take me straight to Sir Josiah, it may not answer, for he may send me away without giving me a hearing. But I must *try* — it is dreadfully important to me, you see — a matter of — yes, in a way, of life and death!"

In spite of some misgivings, Barbara was impressed by the earnestness of this supplication. A tender-hearted girl, she would have yielded at once had she not possessed a lively dread of her Grandsire's anger. She began to explain this, but Susan cut her short.

"Yes, I. know how it is with him, and indeed I don't wish to get you into hot water! I thought perhaps if you could smuggle me into his room —"

Barbara let out an involuntary exclamation of horror.

"Well, get me into the house and show me where it is, then!" amended Susan impatiently. "I can do the rest myself, and he need never know that you had anything to do with it."

"Oh, dear!" sighed Barbara. "I don't wonder that you and Georgiana Eversley are friends. You are really very alike, aren't you?"

"I don't know — perhaps. But will you do it for me, Miss Radley — please? *Please.*"

"Why, of course I would like to be able to help you," replied Barbara, doubtfully. "But — but what about Mama? She is there, too, and I very much doubt if she will consent to allowing someone who is a perfect stranger to my grandfather to enter his room. Besides she dreads anything that's likely to put him in a taking, especially at present — indeed, we all do, and you would, too, did you but know him! Come to think of it, you would be very much better advised, Miss Fyfield, to write him a letter explaining your business. Yes, that would be the thing, don't you agree?"

"No." Susan shook her dark curls. "No, I can't do that. It would be no good at all. I did think you might help me, but I see now that I was mistaken, and I shall have to find some other way." She turned away, her whole body drooping dejectedly. "I am sorry to have troubled you, Miss Radley. Goodbye."

"No, wait a moment!" Barbara moved forward quickly, and seized her arm. "I don't know what this is all about, Miss Fyfield, but one thing I can see is that it matters desperately to you. I will help you, and I think I can see how to get you to my grandfather without Mama knowing anything at all about it — until afterwards," she added, with a barely suppressed shudder. "Follow me."

They went in by the stables, where Barbara handed her horse over to a groom, and then led her companion into the house, through the servants' quarters. Without meeting anyone more formidable than a small housemaid, they rapidly ascended the service staircase to the first floor. There was a door at the end of the staircase; Barbara opened it softly, and peered round it on to the passage beyond. There appeared to be no one about, so she tugged at Susan's gown as a signal, and the two girls quietly eased themselves out into the passage. They tiptoed along it until they came to a point where it widened into a broad landing at the head of a fine flight of stairs leading down to the hall.

Barbara put her mouth close to Susan's ear.

"Grandfather's room is the first door past the staircase," she whispered. "Do be careful, for Mama is sitting in the next one along and may come out at any moment. I will go to her now, and see if I can keep her out of your way."

Susan whispered her thanks, and the two girls fell silent as they sidled quickly past the head of the staircase towards the rooms beyond. When they reached the first door, Barbara gestured towards it, and nodded. Susan reached for the knob with a hand that trembled alarmingly, turned it, and quickly entered the room, before she could change her mind.

Chapter XIX: Susan Finds Her Mother

"Well, come in if you're coming!" ordered a testy voice. "Don't hang about making damnable draughts with that door. Shut it."

Her heart beating fast, Susan obeyed.

"Is it you, East?" went on the voice, in mounting irritation. "What is it now? If it's that damned daughter-in-law of mine wanting to see me again, recommend her to take herself and her whey-faced brat off home at once, before I change my mind and forbid the wedding! Not that I care a button who the silly chit weds! Eh? What's that you say? Speak up, damn you!"

Susan made an inarticulate noise.

The room, in spite of being spacious, was dim. Heavy velour curtains were partly pulled across the windows, excluding the sunlight, and the walls were covered in dark oak panelling. Regardless of the warm summer weather, a small fire burned in the grate. Before this was drawn up a wing chair with its back towards Susan; so that all she could see of its occupant was a white wig which protruded over the top, and a gnarled hand resting on a stick to one side of the chair.

Small though the sound was that she made, it must have told the occupant of the room that decidedly she was not his secretary. He pushed the chair back a little, and began to struggle painfully to his feet with the aid of the stick.

"Plague take it!" he gasped, while this exercise was in progress. "If it isn't one of those cursed females! Whichever it is, ye can take yourself off — get out, I say —"

Susan was trembling violently, but she forced herself to go forward into the room.

"No," she said, between chattering teeth. "I'm not — not —"

He had now succeeded in standing upright, and turned to face her. He was bent with rheumatism, and leaned heavily upon his stick; but she saw that, from the mass of wrinkles which covered his face, a pair of still keen brown eyes studied her carefully.

"No, I can see ye're not," he snapped. "Not blind, yet, y'know — nor wanting in my wits. Dare say ye're a friend of that granddaughter of mine — no business to bring you here — damned impudence! Got into the wrong room, have ye? Well, get out, then. Damned if I won't clear off the whole pack of 'em, now, without waiting till tomorrow. Where's that cursed secretary of mine? He'll see to it."

He put out a shaking hand towards a bell rope that hung close to his chair. Susan fairly flew across the room, placing herself in front of the rope so that he could not reach it without first pushing her aside.

"No, please — please!" she begged, desperation lending her speech. "Don't summon anyone — there's something I must ask you first — in private!"

For a moment, the expression on his face changed from irascibility to surprise. Before he could open his mouth to say anything, Susan rushed on without daring to stop for a moment to consider her words.

"It's my only hope, you see. But I don't know where to begin —" she swallowed — "I live in London with an aunt. At least, I always thought she was an aunt; then one day she told me that she wasn't really related to me at all, but had answered an advertisement in one of the journals for someone to take in a young female child, and bring her up as one of the family. Mrs. Fyfield, this lady's name is, and I am called Susan — but I don't know what my true surname may be — only, I think — I think —"

She paused for breath, and looked anxiously at the old man's face. Apart from a slight narrowing of the dark brown eyes, it gave no sign.

"I think it might be — Radley," she finished. "There is a portrait in one of the downstairs rooms — I haven't seen it myself, but I'm told that it is very like — me —"

The old man's eyes suddenly blazed in his white face.

"Then ye're told lies — damned lies!" he shouted, fiercely. "It's *her* ye favour — that filthy whore!"

Every vestige of colour left Susan's face, and she clutched at the mantelpiece for support.

"Good God, she's going to swoon!" fumed Sir Josiah. He tried to reach the bell rope, but Susan stood swaying before it; so he gave up the attempt, hobbling instead to the door. He threw it wide open, and shouted for assistance.

At once, a number of servants came running. The door next to his opened, and Mrs. Radley and Barbara hastily emerged.

"Whatever is the matter, sir?" asked Mrs. Radley, in alarm. "Are you ill? Shall I send for the doctor?"

"*I'm* all right," he replied, testily, waving a hand to the servants in dismissal. "Just ye two come in here."

Barbara faltered, and hung back; but her mother, although looking far from comfortable herself, was made of sterner stuff. She urged her daughter into the room, and closed the door behind them both.

On catching sight of Susan, she stood stock still, staring. Barbara's face turned from white to red.

"Well, do something, can't ye?" commanded Sir Josiah, impatiently. "Can't have the cursed chit swooning all over the place — get her out of here, and quick! I don't know which of ye's responsible for bringing her here, but I'll know how to deal with ye both, afterwards. Ye'll rue the day, mark my words!"

"You are mistaken, sir," replied Mrs. Radley, in as calm a tone as she could manage. "How this young lady comes to be here, I cannot tell you, but one thing I can say — it is nothing whatever to do with us! Why, neither Barbara nor myself —"

She broke off. She had glanced at her daughter as she mentioned her name, and there was no mistaking the guilty look on Barbara's face. Sir Josiah certainly did not miss it.

"That baggage knows!" He pointed an accusing finger. "Get the girl outside, and then you can come back and damned well give an account of yourself, ma'am!"

"But who is she?" asked Mrs. Radley in a puzzled tone, obediently moving towards Susan, who had abruptly sat down in Sir Josiah's chair, covering her face with her hands.

"She's Susan Fyfield, Mama," put in Barbara, in trembling accents. "We met her at Georgians Eversley's party — she's a school friend of Georgy's —"

"What's that you say?" asked the old man, fixing Barbara with a fierce glare that turned her knees to jelly. "What did you say this chit's name was?"

She repeated the name in a very weak voice.

"That's all ye know about her?" insisted Sir Josiah. "D'ye swear there's nothing else? Answer me!"

He poked her shoulder with a bony finger.

"Yes," stammered Barbara, frightened out of her wits. "Why, grandfather — wh-what else is there to know?"

Mrs. Radley turned suddenly towards him. "Yes — what indeed?" she repeated.

At that moment, Susan stood up and faced the others. She was still pale, but it was evident that she had now got a grip on herself.

"You must tell me now, Sir Josiah," she said, quietly. "I cannot leave without learning the truth. Was your son Robert Radley my father?"

For a moment there was dead silence in the room.

It was broken by the sound of an altercation on the landing. The noise quickly subsided, and the door opened.

A slim, elegant figure slowly entered. He bowed gracefully to the silent company.

"You will, I am sure, pardon my intrusion on this occasion," said the newcomer to Sir Josiah, "although in general I know you do not receive visitors. It must be — let me see — yes, I believe it must be full eighteen years since last we met. How do you do? I fare tolerably well, myself, apart from a touch of my old enemy, the gout. It is pleasant to see you again. And this —" he turned to the ladies, with another gallant bow which belied his years — "is, of course, Mrs. Radley, your fortunate son's wife; and your lovely granddaughter, Miss Barbara Radley — quite one of the Toasts of the Town, I understand." His penetrating dark eyes twinkled at Susan. "And this is my little nymph of the glades, is it not? We met first at my humble villa near the Thames."

"Horry Walpole!" gasped Sir Josiah, his eyes nearly starting from his head. "Good God, what are you doing here? Has everyone gone mad this afternoon?"

"Who shall say?" asked Horace Walpole, gently. "But I fancy I interrupt. Perhaps you were about to tell this young lady —" he indicated Susan with a graceful wave of his hand — "something of importance. Or, my dear fellow, can you have already done so? For I happen to know that she came here with the intention of discovering the truth about her parentage."

"Damn you, Horry, you stuck your long nose into my affairs once before, and you'll not do so again —"

"Long?" Horace Walpole fingered the offending organ, a pained expression on his face. "Surely you wouldn't say it was a long nose, Josiah? You know," he added gently, "I really think you should guard your tongue a little more in front of the ladies."

"I'll damned well do what I choose in my own house! If they don't like it, they can clear out — I've told them so!"

Walpole clicked his tongue deprecatingly. "Dear me, I fear you always were lacking in finesse, Josiah. But have you yet told Miss Susan what she wishes to know?"

"No! Nor will I —"

"Then, my dear fellow, I must. She can no longer remain in ignorance. She is now of marriageable age — in fact, she has a suitor —"

Susan started violently. Horry Walpole turned towards her, a kindly smile on his lips.

"Robert Radley was indeed your father, dear child. He fell in love with someone of whom his father disapproved — she was very young, and as lovely as you are —"

"Lovely!" stormed Sir Josiah, turning the colour of a turkey-cock. "She was a —"

"Silence!" The normally gentle tones hardened. "You have wronged this child sufficiently in keeping from her until now the facts of her parentage —"

"Wronged her? How have I wronged her? She has had her just portion, ain't she? Not a farthing has been kept from her of what would have been my poor boy's fortune, had I not been obliged to cast him off because he was fool enough to succumb to the lures of that scheming hussy, that Jezebel —"

"You have wronged *her*, too. You did so from the first, refusing to believe that there could be any good in the poor little creature, because she was not of your world. And, more lately, you have denied her the small comfort she sought from you in asking for news of her child."

"B'God, you go too far, Walpole!" Sir Josiah almost choked with anger. "Even our old friendship don't give you the right — What use was such a mother to any brat? I gave the creature her choice — either she could leave the child with me, and I would provide for it, or she could take it away, and fend for it herself. She didn't take long to make her decision, I can tell you! Couldn't get rid of the brat soon enough, if you ask me."

Susan winced. Barbara Radley moved to her side, and caught her arm in a comforting clasp.

"It was cruel — cruel!" said Mrs. Radley, with a catch in her voice. "You speak of a choice, but there was no real choice. A young widow, without relatives to assist her, and her way still to make in the world — after all, she was not then eighteen! She knew that most likely she and her baby must starve. Against this, you offered her complete security for the baby and its rightful inheritance, if she would agree to surrender all claim to it, and never try to see it again."

Sir Josiah turned a look of withering scorn on her, and she subsided.

"Ye're a fool, woman — always were! And now get outside, the pack of ye!" He turned to Horace Walpole, and his tone was less belligerent. "If ye've a mind to be civil, Horry, ye can stay and crack a bottle with me, for old time's sake. But I want to hear no more of all this, mark ye! The chit knows now who her father was, and there's an end to the business."

Horry Walpole bowed. "I shall be delighted to accept your invitation, my dear Josiah. But forgive me if I disagree with you when you say that the business we have been discussing is at an end. There is just one other little matter which needs making clear to Miss Susan." He paused, and began to move towards the door. "While she now knows who her father was, she has as yet no notion who is her mother."

Before Sir Josiah could open his mouth to protest, Walpole had reached the door, opened it, and beckoned gracefully to someone who was waiting outside.

She entered the room with professional ease, but her carefully composed face was very pale. Her eyes moved slowly from one to another of the assembly, and came to rest at last on Susan's face.

She gave a deep sigh, and nodded.

"Sure, an' I might have known!" pronounced Maria McCann, with a twisted smile.

The ensuing scene was painful, but mercifully short. Maria McCann and Susan were ordered from the house forthwith, and the Radleys were told that they might go as soon as their packing was completed. All Horace Walpole's charm and tact could not make Sir Josiah relent.

"Not that I would wish to stay," remarked Mrs. Radley, with a shudder, as she and Barbara accompanied Susan and Maria downstairs. "The mere thought of a visit here is enough to induce a fit of the vapours in the ordinary way, let alone under the present circumstances! But when I first came, I thought it only civil to remain for a day or two — after all, Sir Josiah is my husband's father, when all's said and done. However, if he wants us gone, I am sure neither of us is likely to grieve over that!"

"Was he always so — domineering and intolerant?" asked Susan.

"As far back as I can remember," replied Mrs. Radley. "I can recall clearly coming to this house as a bride, and I was quite terrified of him, I assure you, my dear! But I think he did become worse after —"

Her voice tailed away, and she looked at Maria.

"It might have been so different," said Maria, in her lilting voice. "If only he could have brought himself to accept me, we could all have gone on very comfortably together, could we not, ma'am? But, there!" She shrugged. "I was an actress, and he was so certain that I was only after Rob's fortune."

"I might have tried to help you," said Mrs. Radley, in a conscience-stricken tone. "I see that now, though it all appeared in a different light at the time. I was young, and terrified of my father-in-law. Besides —" she hesitated — "you must forgive me for saying this, but I could not be perfectly sure —"

"That I was not after Rob's money, as your father-in-law believed?" said Maria, swiftly, with a little twisted smile that went straight to Susan's heart. "No, of course — how should you be? After all, I was an actress."

"I have since come to realize," said Mrs. Radley, with an effort, "that they may not be so very different from the generality of women." She broke off, as she fancied she heard sounds from upstairs. "But I dare not stay," she finished, hurriedly. "I collect you came here with Mr. Walpole, and as he is to stay the night, perhaps you would care to accept a seat in my coach back to Town? I will call at the Black Horse to take you up on my way through the village. We shall be leaving within the hour. Shall I ask one of the servants to escort you back to the inn?"

Susan and Maria unanimously declined this offer, but said that they might very well be glad of seats in the Radleys' coach.

"And ourselves with the undeniable right to ride in it," said Maria, with her irrepressible humour, as they started off down the drive towards the gates.

"I was never so glad of anything in my life," said Susan, impetuously, "as when I heard Mr. Walpole say that you and my father —"

She broke off, realizing with dismay that she had been on the verge of an indiscretion. But Maria McCann only chuckled.

"That we were married in due form, with fitting rites and ceremonies? Of course you were relieved, my dear. But you had nothing to fear, either way, for your father was a gentleman, which is all that counts in Polite Society."

"It is all so strange," said Susan, after a moment. "Tell me, what kind of man was my father?"

"A young girl's dream," replied Maria, her blue eyes deepening. "Just as Beau Eversley is, though physically they are not alike."

Susan coloured.

Maria looked at her thoughtfully for a moment, then went on, "He had that wonderful golden hair of the Radleys, and deep brown eyes, like glossy chestnuts. Whenever he came into a room, everyone noticed him at once." She sighed. "I have never met another like him."

"Never?" Susan found it impossible to repress the question.

"No." Maria stole a second glance at her daughter, and smiled wistfully. "Sure, an' I know what you're thinking, child. But although I'll confess I did admire the Beau, and always enjoyed his company, there was never anything between us that need vex your pretty head for a moment. Our friendship was of the most platonic — I swear it," she finished, in a serious tone.

"I'm sure Mr. Eversley's affairs are no concern of mine," replied Susan, stiffly.

"Hoity toity!" said Maria, mockingly. "You've changed then, my child, for I remember the first time we met it was plain to see that you were head over ears in love with the gentleman."

Susan elevated her nose, and tossed her black curls disdainfully.

"There!" exclaimed Maria, in wonder. "When you do that, even I can see that you resemble me!"

Susan looked at her doubtfully for a moment, then gave a little laugh. Maria joined in readily.

"Tell me about your marriage to my father," said Susan, sobering again. "I managed to learn something from what was said at Pyncott Place, but I would like to know all about it."

So, as they walked together back to the village inn, Maria told her new-found daughter the full story of this young couple who had fallen in love and married in spite of parental disapproval, and afterwards found themselves in dire financial straits.

"Your father was too proud to accept help from his relatives and friends," related Maria, "and I had none to turn to, except those of the play company who had come with me from Ireland; and they were too hard pressed themselves to help. Besides, we were obliged to flee from London, for fear of what your grandfather might do. He was vicious in his wrath. We had a little money between us, at first, and we lived — oh, so happily!" She sighed, and then added, "Until it was all gone."

"Then what did you do?" asked Susan, softly. Her imagination was at work, putting herself in her mother's place, conjuring up afresh the emotions of that younger Maria, who had braved everything to be with her true love.

Maria's face saddened. "Rob tried to find work, but it was almost impossible. He had been trained for nothing but the life of a gentleman. Sometimes he would tramp for miles in the hope of finding employment, only to be turned away as unsuitable at the end of it. He would have tried anything — tutor, groom, farm labourer — his spirit was boundless; but people were suspicious of his gentlemanly looks and tones, and when they asked for references, what could he say? And his pride wouldn't permit that I should seek employment of any kind — though I did manage to earn the odd shilling without his knowledge, now and then."

"He — was killed in an accident, I think?" said Susan, gently.

Maria nodded, and turned her face away. "He was knocked down by a carriage when he was returning from one of his long tramps in search of work. They brought him home to the cottage where we lodged, but he never recovered consciousness." Her voice dropped so that Susan could scarcely hear it. "He died the next day."

Susan caught her mother's hand, and pressed it in silent sympathy. Maria was silent for a time.

"After I recovered from the shock," she went on, presently, in a stronger tone, "I approached Sir Josiah, to see if he would help me support the child I was soon to bear. I could not have done it for myself, but I had you to think of. His answer you already know, for it was mentioned just now at Pyncott Place. As my sister-in-law said, I had no real choice. How could I choose poverty and privation for my child, when it could have wealth and security if only I would give it up to Sir Josiah completely?"

She looked at Susan for support, and the girl nodded silently.

"I kept my part of the bargain," went on Maria, "hard though it was. They took you away when you were only three weeks old, and I returned to my own country. I never tried to see you — until now, when I am about to marry again. He is a good man in my own profession, and I know we shall go on comfortably together. But first, I had to assure myself that my child was well and happy; and so I came to beg Sir Josiah to tell me where I might find you — only to see you, not to disclose myself to you as your mother. But he refused."

"He is a brute!" exclaimed Susan, fiercely.

"Perhaps." Maria shrugged helplessly. "No doubt he felt he was acting for the best."

They fell silent for a while, then Susan said, diffidently, "So you are returning to Ireland. You — you don't wish — that I should accompany you?"

Maria stopped in her tracks, and threw her arms impetuously about her daughter.

"Bless you!" she said, with a break in her voice. "But no, my love, it would not answer at all, at all! We have been too long apart, I think, for that. You are now at an age when a girl wants to discard her mother, not draw closer to her; and our ways of life have been so very different! Besides, there are those —" She released Susan, and gave her a knowing smile — "who have quite different plans for your future, I collect."

Susan coloured a little. "Perhaps you are right," she admitted. "But, all the same, I don't intend that you should vanish from my life completely! You can have no notion how comforting it is to discover that there is someone in the world who is really and truly my own! But what should I do about my name?" she finished, as another thought struck her. "Ought I to call myself Radley?"

"No," said Maria, decidedly. "I have no wish for you to become a subject for gossip. The Radleys themselves will know the truth, and that is all that matters. Besides," she added, with a roguish glance, "you will soon enough be changing your name, in any event."

"I wish you will not say such foolish things! But I am not sorry to find that I am related to Barbara Radley, for I think her a very good kind of girl, don't you?"

Maria assented.

"You know," went on Susan, shyly, "there was a time when — when Beau Eversley —"

"Admired Barbara?" finished Maria, looking searchingly at Susan's face. "Yes, so I have heard. What if he did once fleetingly admire your cousin — and even your Mama? It's all in the family." She broke off, then quoted in her soft, lilting voice: "'*So all their praises are but prophecies, Of this our time, all you prefiguring* —' Doesn't that explain it, my love? No one but Shakespeare can put things so well. Barbara and I have acted as your understudies, but now you take the stage."

"I wish you will not talk so — it cannot be anything but nonsense!"

"Remarkably serious nonsense, when a man is prepared to dash all over the countryside in order to discover the facts of a girl's parentage! Only consider what he has done today — he was responsible for bringing Horry Walpole and myself here, you know."

"As to that," replied Susan, slowly, "in a sense, I forced him into helping me. Oh, I think I had best tell you everything!" she concluded. "After all, you are my mother."

Maria listened to the account that followed with a gradually widening smile of appreciation on her generous mouth.

"Capital!" she exclaimed, when Susan had finished. "My poor child, you are every bit as impetuous as your parents were before you! God grant a happier outcome for you — and I truly believe it will be so. For you will never persuade me that a man will go to so much trouble except for the girl he truly loves! I am no judge of the matter if he isn't head over ears, and thinking of no one but yourself at this very moment!"

"But that's just it," replied Susan, in a despondent tone. "Georgy is of your opinion, too; but she warned me not to depend on his attachment —" with a blush — "lasting any length of time, for she says he is the most shocking flirt, and always in love with someone or other! And indeed, ma'am, everyone knows that to be true — it is common gossip."

"Gossip!" exclaimed Maria, scornfully. "I have been about the world a good bit, my love, and I think I know how to rate gossip! But I see you are not convinced —" as Susan shook her head. "Well, then, let me tell you something, my little Sue, about gentlemen of Beau Eversley's stamp. They will admire many females in their time, paying court to these ladies by bringing pretty gifts and taking some trouble — not too much! — in gratifying their foolish whims. But something is always expected in return —" there was a bitter note in her voice — "and should the return disappoint the so generous donor, then the court is transferred to another, possibly more appreciative, lady. But when a man truly loves, child —" her tone changed to one of tenderness — "he will offer all he has, though it be nothing in the eyes of the world; and he will expect from the lady nothing in return save what she freely chooses to give."

Susan was silent. Maria looked along the road; the inn was in sight, and two figures were standing in the small forecourt, watching their approach. After a moment, Susan looked up and caught sight of them, too.

"Oh, Maria!" she exclaimed, in sudden alarm. "I had not realized when you said that Beau Eversley had brought you here — but, of course, he is waiting for us at the Black Horse! And George, too — I don't know if yon found out, but he brought me to Middlesex in his curricle! But the thing is, that I always feel so — so uncomfortable nowadays whenever they are together, for George has taken it into his head that he admires me — though I think it is only calf-love, in spite of what my friend Georgiana says — and then —" her voice faltered — "and then there is Beau! Oh, Maria, what am I to do?"

"Do, Susan?" replied Maria, in a rallying tone. "Why, straighten your bonnet, compose yourself, and walk on to face your audience like the splendid little actress you might have been!"

Chapter XX: Dinner at Strawberry Hill

The footman moved to fill Horace Walpole's glass with his favourite drink, ice water.

"You'll take some more wine, Hugh?" pressed his host, hospitably. "Do you think perhaps the ladies might be persuaded —?"

Across the table, Beau Eversley's eyes met Susan's. She smiled ruefully.

"No wine for me, I thank you, sir," she replied, demurely. "It — it does not suit me."

"I am delighted to hear that, my dear Miss Susan, for it is one more thing which we have in common. I doubt —" he concluded, turning to the two other ladies who made up the party seated at the table, "if my old friends Agnes and Mary will be tempted, either."

Both the Misses Berry, who lived in a cottage on Horry Walpole's estate and were often asked to the house to dine, politely declined.

"In that case," went on Horry, smiling, "I will order coffee. And after we have all enjoyed a comfortable chat over it, perhaps you, dear boy —" turning to Hugh — "will be so good as to do the honours for me, and show Miss Susan the gardens." His lively dark eyes rested on Susan, with a twinkle in them. "You know, my dear, it has been so great a pleasure to invite you here, and show you all my little treasures. I was quite determined I should do it, one day, ever since that time when you first paid me a visit and were obliged to leave — ah — so hurriedly."

Susan choked a little, and tried hard not to look at Beau Eversley. "You are very good, sir," she managed to say.

Her host bowed.

"It is an easy matter to be good to one so charming," he replied, gallantly. "Do you not agree, Hugh?"

This time, Susan could not avoid the Beau's steady gaze. She coloured a little under it, veiling her eyes with her long dark lashes.

"I do indeed, sir. In fact, I have frequently made that very remark myself to Miss Susan."

"I feel sure you must have done so, my dear fellow." Horry was clearly enjoying himself. "In spite of the shaggy hair and informal mode of dress favoured by the man of today, at heart he is, I believe, very much as he always was. In short, while young ladies are beautiful and charming, young men will still delight in telling them so."

Fortunately, the coffee arrived at this point; and, to Susan's relief, the conversation took a less personal turn. When the meal at last drew to a close, however, Susan and Beau Eversley were firmly but courteously sent on their way to the gardens alone.

At first, they found little to say to each other. Beau Eversley made some attempt to "do the honours", as Horry Walpole had put it; but his comments on the various natural beauties they encountered in their stroll drew forth scant response from the lady.

The first remark she volunteered was when they were walking under the lilacs. She paused, looking ruefully up at the trees.

"All the bloom's gone," she said wistfully. "And they were so lovely that day — I shall always remember them."

His green-flecked eyes looked into hers, and she noticed that the customary twinkle had vanished.

"The day that you leapt into my life?" he asked, softly. "You will always remember the lilacs — and I shall always remember — you."

"It's no use to make pretty speeches," said Susan, attempting a light tone. "I am not deceived, sir!"

"Why should you think I wish to deceive you?"

Her eyes dropped before his intense gaze, but she tried to keep up a pretence of levity.

"Because it is a game you play — and remarkably well, too!"

"This is no game, Susan. I was never more in earnest, I assure you."

He made a movement towards her, but she stepped back as if in alarm.

"No — please — pray say no more —"

A look of mortification crossed his face. "Very well, if that is what you wish."

He paused a moment, waiting for her to speak, but she said nothing.

"I saw George before I came here," he continued, watching her slightly averted face. "He told me that he had made you an offer of marriage — and that you had refused him."

She smiled, and shook her head. "Silly boy! At present he fancies that he cares for me, but it is just because I am the first girl he has ever really noticed. Why, it is obvious that he really thinks more of his horses than he does of me! I wish you could have seen the fuss he made when one of them injured itself on our way to Pyncott Place. He could scarcely bring himself to speak to me civilly, and I could see that he thought it was all my fault. No, I am sure it is all fancy — if he can recall my very name six months hence, I confess I shall be amazed!"

"No doubt you are an authority in these matters," the Beau said, dryly.

"Well, yes, I am," she answered, impetuously. "You see, George isn't the first to suffer from — feelings of the kind. I, too —"

"Yes?" He waited a moment, then saw that she had no intention of saying more. "You were perhaps about to say," he suggested, diffidently, "that you, too, once entertained the same feeling towards George?"

"No — yes — no, not that, exactly," she stammered, losing her poise, and recovering it again with difficulty. "When I saw — that he admired me — I was a little drawn to him, if I am honest — even though I realized all along that his feelings for me would not last."

"And so you refused him, even though you —" he broke off, and repeated her words in an expressionless tone — "felt yourself drawn to him?"

"You don't understand. I felt a kindness for him, that is all. It was partly because I thought myself so — so much of an outcast at that time, without either name or family; and I was ready to be grateful to anyone who would show the least interest in me."

"Believe me," he said, seriously, "I do understand. Yet there were others who had certainly not lost interest in you, I believe."

"You mean my aunt, and Georgiana —"

"Certainly. I also mean myself."

She made a little nervous movement of her hands. "You — you were very kind to me, sir — much kinder than I deserved, I realize that."

"Why did you run away, Susan?" he asked, moving nearer to her. "Didn't you know that I intended to make our fictitious betrothal a reality when I should see Mr. Watson on the following day?"

She nodded unhappily. "Oh, yes. But how could I let you do such a thing for me? Beau Eversley to become betrothed to a — a nobody! It was unthinkable!"

"Your unselfishness does you credit," he said, gently. "In such a situation, you might have been pardoned for taking the easy way, and accepting the security of my name."

"I'm not unselfish," she replied, in a low tone. "I was — tempted. But — I knew it would not do. You see, you did not —"

She broke off, and turned her head away to hide the tears which sprang to her eyes.

"Yes? What did I not do, Susan?"

He took her hands gently in his. She made a feeble effort to release them, then was still.

"You — did not love me." He had to bend his head to catch the words. "And I —"

"My dear —" he raised her hands to his lips. "We are not always privileged to know the truth about ourselves and our motives. I thought — and evidently you did, too — that I regarded you as a rather tiresome little friend of my sister who had got herself into a scape, and must be helped out of it."

She drew her hands away, clasping them firmly together before her to try and still their trembling.

"It was much later," he went on, fixing his eyes on her downcast head, "that I came to realize how all along I had been falling in love with you."

"No." She raised her head at that, looking almost defiantly into his face. "It wasn't love, but the kind of — of infatuation that you have felt for many others. Don't think that while I was in Town I didn't hear gossip. On every side, I heard what an incorrigible flirt Beau Eversley is! There were dozens of females whom you had first admired, and later lost all interest in — among them even my own relatives, though I didn't know then that we were related — Barbara Radley, and — and —"

"And Maria?" he finished, smoothly. "Tell me — I know you had a very little time together before she left for Ireland — but did she speak to you at all on this subject?"

"Yes, she did." Susan's tone was quieter, now.

"Then she must have told you of the essentially platonic nature of our friendship."

"It was not *your* fault that it was platonic, though!" said Susan, fiercely, shaking her dark curls in a sudden gust of anger.

"You are jealous — my sweet life, you are jealous!" He took her in his arms, and she could feel her anger melting away. "Now I know what I had hardly dared to hope — that you, too, love me."

"Always," whispered Susan, turning her face up to his. "Always. At first, it was only a schoolgirl's dream — but later, when I had come to know you, it changed to something deeper. And after that, all I wanted in the world was for you to love me — and it seemed that you never could, for one reason or another!"

"There have never been any reasons strong enough to stop me," he murmured, his lips very close to hers. "Do you think, dearest, I might kiss you now? After all, we've been betrothed for a very long time."

A NOTE TO THE READER

If you have enjoyed the novel enough to leave a review on **Amazon** and **Goodreads**, then we would be truly grateful.

Sapere Books is an exciting new publisher of brilliant fiction and popular history.

To find out more about our latest releases and our monthly bargain books visit our website: **saperebooks.com**

Printed in Great Britain
by Amazon